Priscilla,

WATILI

— ENJOY —

THE NATIVE AMERICAN SLAVE HEROINE

ANTHONY GARCIA

Copyright © 2017 by Anthony Garcia.

All rights reserved. No part of this publication may be reproduced, distributed or transmitted in any form or by any means, including photocopying, recording, or other electronic or mechanical methods, without the prior written permission of the publisher, except in the case of brief quotations embodied in critical reviews and certain other noncommercial uses permitted by copyright law.

Anthony Garcia/Watili The Native American Slave Heroine
Printed in the United States of America

Manuscript Editor: Adrianna Veatch
Back Cover Photographer: Soledad Garcia

This is a work of fiction. Names, characters, places, and incidents are a product of the author's imagination. Locales and public names are sometimes used for atmospheric purposes. Any resemblance to actual people, living or dead, or to businesses, companies, events, institutions, or locales is completely coincidental.

Watili The Native American Slave Heroine/Anthony Garcia -- 1st ed.

For more information or to contact the author visit www.Watili.com

ISBN 978-0-9903739-3-3 Print Edition

Library of Congress Control Number: 2017906596

Contents

1. Introduction 1
2. Apache-Mescaleros Enslave Parussi Band Members 5
3. Watili the Slave Maid 19
4. Watili's Discovery of Escalante-Dominguez Map and Journal 25
5. Pact for Watili's Freedom 31
6. Journey on El Camino Real (The Royal Road to Santa Fe) 39
7. Concealed Journey to Obtain Gold Dust in the
   Wayatoya Mountains 43
8. Battle for La Veta Pass 55
9. The Journey to Watili's Village 61
10. Encounter with Yutas Barbones (Bearded Utes) 77
11. Colorado River—Passage to the Pacific 83
12. Watili's Village - The Parussi 95
13. Watili the Leader 107
15. Final Chapter 111

Dedication

This is a mirror book. It tells a story from the inside-out, sharing a story of Watili, her life experiences and her native point of view. Most books written on historical fiction are written from the prospective of the outside-in, a window looking in, an outsider telling their views of a community looking through a window of the past, yet never personally experiencing what the characters have felt.

Very little is written about the first American territory contact between Natives and the Spanish northern most empire in the time frame of 1775. This book was written to share of these indigenous people and to recognize the fragile independent villages that populated the Rocky Mountains and how they lived in Oneness with nature and feared exploitation of their lives.

The real lesson of this book is Watili, as she shares her native understanding of the Oneness between mankind and nature. How the Creator-Higher Being God longs for this relationship to be understood and his/her lands not be ravaged or polluted.

I wish to Thank the proof readers and editors that have worked on this book with me, a heartfelt "Brazo y Gracias" I send to you.

I dedicate this book to those educators and administrators that possess the understanding to recognize the paradigm shift of intellect to recognize organic contributions of our world and to make available the contributions of the native community to the fabric of these United of States of America we live within. To recognize the sacrifice and Oneness of the entire Native Indigenous community is what will make America Great Again.

Un beso al bien futuro a mis hijos, EG, AG, ABG, SG.

Anthony Garcia

Artist's Acknowledgement

Ernie Gallegos

When I was asked to complete a drawing of Watili, I was moved by this young women that would be uprooted into another world and enslaved into an environment of what she had no understanding or personal relationship with. I immediately related to the young native women's plight.

I was 21 years old and was drafted to take part in the Vietnam conflict. I left the comforts of my small town and home in northern Colorado and was asked to serve my country in a far distant land that I had no understanding or personal relationship with.

I think it was near the town of Tan An, Vietnam, we were on patrol near small villages when I first heard my fellow grunts men use the term, "when I get back to the world". At first I did not understand what that term meant. That evening under the stars, I realized that I was taken from my world and sent to serve in a place that was almost impossible to explain.

In my drawing of Watili, I draw from my knowledge that she was taken from "her world" and placed in an environment that I am sure she could not understand, yet she knew she had to survive. Her survival instinct was to survive to see her family again in her home village of Parussi, my instinct was to survive both physically and mentally.

Look at Watili's eyes, you will see the vacant look in her eyes, the traumatic shock and pain of what she felt. She was traumatized and yet she showed her toughness to endure such an experience that maybe no one would ever understand.

The Mine symbol on her neck is placed there in remembrance of her brother Peregrue, he also was taken captive and coerced to work in the mines only to never be seen again.

I hope you enjoy my drawing.

Ernie Gallegos

www.GallegosArt.tripod.com

Specialist Ernie Gallegos was awarded the Silver Star metal, the third highest award for combat valor in Vietnam and the Army Commendation Medal with "V" device for valorous actions in direct contact with an enemy for his service to his country.

Author's Note

The defining image of Watili is that of a young native person that believes in herself and in her heart she comprehends that relationship between mankind, nature and the Creator.

Watili endures the 700 mile forced walk into a world she does not comprehend, leaving behind a truly enjoyable life and healthy environment to be enslaved as a domestic servant to live in a quiet fear of her future.

Yet she shows no hate for either the Spanish or the Apache Mescalero that enslaved her for she possessed a grounded common sense and belief that someday she will return to her world of the Parussi band.

As the story develops, the real lesson is how Watili maintains her native understanding, the Oneness between mankind and nature and how Creator-higher Being God wants this relationship to exist for the land to not be exploited.

Watili sharing of her healing capabilities by use of plants and prayers to the Creator demonstrate the interdependent Oneness between faith and nature. The Native soul is entwined with nature and this mutual dependency of the Creator-Higher Being God created for this Oneness to exist.

The young native girl shares, Earth is our mother, Whatever befalls Earth, befalls the son and daughter of Earth.

We have reached a point that the Earth has been exploited and the Oneness-the credence of mankind and nature has been frayed and on the verge of collapse.

To return to this Oneness, one must return to the Native Soul that has long been set aside but has not disappeared. As Watili said:

All things are connected, like the blood that unites one family. All things are connected. We did not weave the web of life. We are merely a strand in it. Whatever we do to the web, we do to ourselves

Introduction

Five years after Don Bernardo Miera y Pacheco accompanied the first Dominguez-Escalante expedition into American southwest in 1776, the map maker-cartographer Don Bernardo decides to return without the consent of the Spanish Crown into the region in his quest to locate gold and silver mines. A devout Christian and slaver, Don Bernardo sought to comprehend powerful lessons he missed during of the first expedition, an insight that native peoples retained and an allure to obtain this wisdom by rejoining with these native lands.

Accompanying the mapmaker was native Ute Indian slave maid named Watilit, a young intelligent and independent persona that possessed knowledge of silver and gold veins near her home rancheria-village of Parussi located in present southwest Utah. Yet a forerunner to the insightful Curandera-folk healer, a figure that will be ever present in these lands.

What Watili really possessed was the graceful understanding of the relationship of Oneness between nature and spirituality. This lesson to be shared with Don Bernardo and the newly found friend on the journey, Cibolero the Spanish Buffalo Hunter. The new European arrivals are taught to understand how nature provides life-spirituality-healing in ways they never knew existed and to find their organic selves in the process.

Retracing the original journey via the detailed map into the delicate and unspoiled mountain lands provided a rare glimpse into the life and battles among native Indians that depended heavily upon nature to provide the nourishment to endure life in "wilderness" as Don Bernardo preferred to describe such pristine environment.

Maps are funny thing, they map tell you of the route and length of a journey, yet also disclose of locations that are not intended to be shared. Don Bernardo's map of native camps, hunting grounds, village movement corridors within valleys provided a detailed and educated process for exploiters to locate the fragile native peoples that lived within this untouched lands.

Join this reading, as you explore two points of view into undeveloped and unspoiled lands as they collide to share the understanding of the Oneness of nature and spirituality. You will also preview the development of Watili into the Native American Slave Heroine.

The saying, "you do not know yourself, until you know your past," is never more prevalent and shared to those wanting to grasp of the Oneness that eludes many a western mind.

Dominguez-Escalante 1776 Expedition Map

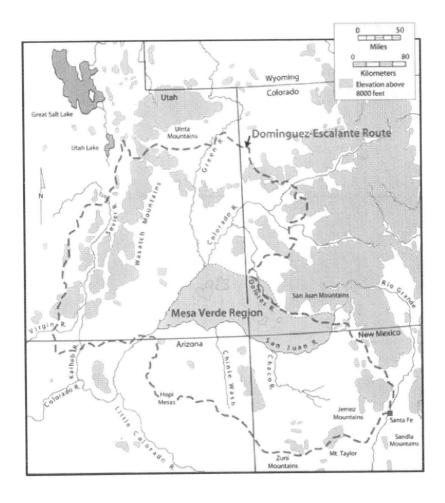

APACHE MESCALEROS SLAVERS CAPTURE PARUSSI BAND MEMBERS

Apaches Mescaleros traveled forty-five miles a day in search of captives to enslave, using the map and journal they had acquired. They had not yet come across a significant band to attack, though they had seen several small, individual groups who would scatter at the sight of an *Apache* and his horse.

The *Apaches* were prairie natives, accustomed to eating the red meat of the buffalo. The heavy bone and muscle structure was evidence these natives had access to protein on a consistent basis; also, their sun baked dark complexions showed they came from a territory of much sun.

Following the river flowing from the west, they continued uphill to the *San Clemente* River (present-day Meeker, *Colorado*). As luck would have it, they came across the *Parussi* Band they had pursued, following the detailed map of Don Bernardo Pacheco y Miera.

The forward scouts returned wide-eyed with the look of finding riches: the riches of locating an unsuspecting native band. All horsemen dismounted and quietly began to walk along the slender canyon, until in the distance, *chozas* (small huts made of reeds) outlined the landscape in the early afternoon light. They walked further towards the village, so as not to startle the dwellers or their dogs.

Upon quietly entering the village, the *Apaches* mounted their horses and raised their buffalo-femur hatches, with the rounded clubs pointed outward to crack at anyone in sight.

The Day Before the Raid

The day before Watili's kidnapping, the fourteen-year-old was awoken by her grandfather early in the morning. Two days prior, he had asked her parents' permission to take her out hunting for medicinal herbs along the big river. Watili had been so excited. Now, Grandfather knelt down, opened the *choza*, and gently squeezed the toe of his sleeping granddaughter. Watili was sleeping with the dark-haired doll her father had carved for her, lying at her side. She felt her toe being squeezed and smiled, leapt from her deer-skin blanket, and then dressed quickly so as not to make her grandfather wait.

As she came out of the *choza* into the cool mountain air, the sun was rising above the top of the snowy peaks. Her grandfather smiled at her as he held out the dry deer bladders they would fill with various herbs on their short journey to the big river. They walked silently through the village so as not to awaken others, but also to absorb the Oneness with Nature.

"Listen in your heart and look with your soul, little granddaughter," the old man whispered into her ear. "The daybreak awakens Nature and giving life for us to feed upon is as the Creator intended."

They crossed the smaller, flowing *rito* (creek) kneeling with cupped hands to drink a little water. How could little Watili have known the tranquility of her world would be shattered the next day, and her life changed forever? Today, the calm of the cooling water, and its peaceful, bubbling song was all she knew. Hand-in-hand with her grandfather, she walked through the untouched forest as birds chirped "good morning". Rabbits began their daily search for food, squirrels chattered at them from the trees, leaves uncurled in the warm sunlight, and unblemished air welcomed the walkers to their destiny.

They soon arrived at the big river a few miles from the village; the grandfather strolled sideways down the embankment with Watili following closely behind.

Grandfather smiled at the river and what Nature had provided that day. "These waters provide all of the healing a village needs to survive. This early summer, the blossoms from the plants will provide herbs we need to heal any illness or disease. Our people have always depended on Earth to provide these remedies and today," he knelt to examine a plant, "they are in perfect bloom."

The grandfather handed her a few of the bladders with deer strings attached to hang upon her shoulder. As she followed him, he began to carefully gather plants, roots and blossoms in his hand. As he carefully pulled each plant, he would say a prayer of thanks to *Senawa* for the blessings that enabled him to heal his village, as he carefully placed each herb into a separate bladder.

Watili felt a seed of knowledge uncurling in her *frente* (forehead) at the sight of her grandfather's wisdom and prayers. Her heart felt open to learning as she watched the herbs flutter down into the bladders, and she dropped to her knees beside her grandfather.

"Thank you, *Senawaha*," she said, joining her grandfather in prayer. The education of Watili continued.

"Thank you, *Senawaha*," she said. Grandfather smiled as her young voice joined his prayer, knowing he was educating her in the craft of healing. He continued, "This bitterroot with the purple flower, when cleaned and mixed with this leaf, heals sore throats. This blossom, dried and mashed and drunk with hot water, will cure a cold." The grandfather spoke reverently as he shared this knowledge with Watili.

This was the alchemy outsiders never understood: the Oneness in the form of prayer that extracted health from Earth and Nature, a healing that the Creator provided.

With the bladders full of healing remedies, the pair returned to the village. A good morning's efforts came to an end as Watili ducked into her *choza* and found her doll. She began telling her favorite doll about her morning and what she had learned. The doll had been carved out of soft white aspen wood, and darkened with oil from the skin of a river-fish. It had been whittled with strong Native features like a rugged nose, wide jaw, and high cheek bones; the hair was made of dyed-black corn silk attached to the head by yucca sap; the body was varnished with piñon nut oil and dressed with a hare fur *tunico* (dress).

Watili's mother listened and watched this little interchange, smiling and acknowledging the wisdom her own astute father had bestowed to her daughter.

Outside, Watili's mother prepared food for her and her grandfather to eat: *atole* (corn meal with wild berries and deer fat, to add a creamy texture), and a sweetener of bark gum.

"Oh Mother, thank you! My favorite, atole!" cried Watili, as she quickly swallowed two whole platefuls from her wooden trencher. As a side dish, the mother boiled the sweet-tasting deer tongue, always a young person's favorite meat.

After eating, Watili ran to her *choza* to collect the doll her father had made her. She walked out of the *choza* to find her friends, proudly holding her doll in her hand. This was not a work day for her. She strolled past villagers skinning deer and rabbits; young men hanging freshly caught and cleaned trout stomach on sticks as the warm sun and air dried their bodies; mothers and daughters gathering wild berries, chokecherries, and greens in the distance.

She finally found her girlfriends. They played with their dolls, ran to the *rito*, and raced through the mud. They were soon joined by the boys of the village. The girls set their dolls to the side and looked for sticks and a round hemp ball, and soon the children began playing a form of lacrosse. Watili excelled in this game and demonstrated her competitive spirit against the boys, scoring point after point in a make shift hemp net.

Finally, other young boys caught up to the girls playing lacrosse and chased them, hoping to pry them away from their friends to spend some alone time with the girls. The young girls naturally do what they always do: formed a group and kept the boys away. Some things never change.

It was late afternoon when Watili returned to her parents *choza*. She'd worked up quite an appetite playing with her friends.

"Mama, what is for dinner?" a hungry Watili asked her mother.

"I am boiling water. Can you help me chop up these plants and roots?" the mother asked from the *choza*.

Watili saw the vegetables she was to cut lying in a bundle next to the fire; she rinsed her hands and used a sharpened shale knife her father had crafted to begin cutting various roots, wild grass rice, and green spinach. Inside the pot was a thick deer bone, its shaft split open to permit the marrow and bone to dissolve and add flavor to the water. Her mother came out from the *choza* with soaked corn, the kernels now open, and cut up pieces of dried deer kidney. Stooping over the fire, she added these and a handful of sunflower seeds to the boiling water. Lastly, she added deer fat and stirred the soup before calling her children and husband to eat this organic paleo meal.

After dinner, nighttime crept quickly over the village as they sat around a small fire. The time Watili spent with her family was a special time. The fire provided a place to giggle and share stories of the day. Her brother Peregrue, a year older, talked about the predatory-natured falcons that would dive boldly to earth, and yank a garden snake from under a dry log, then fly up to the nest to feed it to their chirping young. Living with and witnessing the Oneness with Nature of this lifestyle cannot be duplicated nor reinvented.

The family retired to sleep in the *choza* that housed Watili's father, mother, brother, and herself. The serene sound of the cool *rito* was the only sound in the village. Bright stars lit the dark background of the universe; the stuttering breeze moved the hanging tree limbs to and fro, and yet there was no suggestion life would forever change in a few hours.

This tranquility and calm would soon be shattered and eternally a permanent memory, changed by a map, big dogs (horses), and the absolute greed of advancing technology.

With thump of hoofs clamoring on moist ground, they attacked every *choza*. The villagers scattered and were easy pray for the horseman and their hatches. The first six horseman attacked every person and hit them square on the head to daze and knock them to the ground. The second group of six *Apaches* grabbed, dazed, and forced them into groups of ten, continually pounding their head and shoulders until they were forced to the ground.

In all, sixty Natives were captured by the *Apaches*. Old people who appeared unable to a handle a treacherous walk to Janos (outside of *Chihuhaua, Mexico*) were removed from the circle. There were four groups of ten left. A few of the villagers escaped into the woods, where horses could not freely run them down.

Young and narrow aspen lodge poles were cut down and the slender pieces of strip bark were removed. They separated the young men from the women. First, he men's hands were tied very tightly along the wrists. Then they were forced to stand up according to height, and the pole was placed between two of them on their shoulders.

Then the aspen bark was tied along their necks and onto the lodge pole.

The women were treated the same way. This was all completed in less than one hour. Quite an efficient system: this schema cultivated after many a raiding party. This slavery capture would forever change the fate of the calm oneness of Nature and the *Parussi* clan.

To prevent any possible resistance by the older family members, they were removed and placed aside as they stood watching these events. The horseman again attacked this group, knocking them all to the ground and challenging anyone to raise from the ground. Then, using their bone hatches, the *Apache* drove their forty neck-bound captives out of the village, to whereabouts unknown.

Confusion set upon the captives as they began their march. Open wounds on their heads and shoulders were not attended to, so blood was flowing from their crowns and shoulders. The captives began to cry for their mothers and fathers. The older people and parents raised their hands and cried their children's name from the ground, powerless to rescue their loved ones. Yet it did not matter. The horsemen had their day and knew a payday would result from their efforts.

They navigated back to *Janos*, using the map to march at night, leaving two horsemen to lag behind and slowly follow the group one half mile behind, to ensure no rescue attempts were made by the *Parussi* Band.

The *Apaches* wore thick overcoat buffalo robes as coats, thick long sleeve shirts, leggings made of buffalo skin, and rawhide ankle high moccasins. The prairie natives had a distinct advantage of accessing the value the buffalo provided. The cool mountain evenings did not affect the *Apaches*: their thick clothing saw to that.

Watili was the tender age of fourteen when she was captured. Slender and strong with bright eyes, she grasped and understood all that was shared with her. She could run like a deer with a smile that enlightened the evening sky. The granddaughter of the prominent medicine man, she frequently traveled with him for medicinal plants and learned to dry and mix these plants for the remedies needed for life-healing in the primeval forest. She learned to heal ailments and bone fractures just from native plants. This was in a time when a broken bone could mean life or death if not addressed immediately.

Watili, with dried blood on her forehead and cheek, could barely see her brother who was tied to the men's group, separated far in front of the caravan. She wondered if he knew she too was a captive. They could not make eye contact. Traveling at night through sagebrush and rough terrain, all the captive's feet were cut and bruised, and blood flowed into their toes. They finally came to stop and were forced to sit down with the lodge poles attached between their shoulders. None were permitted to move, and all urinated upon themselves with fear. Two fires were lit to warm the night air and kept burning until dawn to ensure the value of healthy slaves would be maintained. This *Parussi* band was quite a capture: premium trade value next to a young horse at the slave trade market. The journal and map composed by Don Bernardo made this all possible.

Early the next morning, they marched again. Only the youthfulness of these captives would keep them alive. On the evening of the second day, the *Apaches* located a river with low, wide banks. Since the *Apaches* language was *Athabaskan*, not a single *Parussi* understood them, so the *Apaches* used only strict hand signs to provide instructions to the group. Each captive, one by one, was loosened at the neck. The heavy hatch led each one to the river where they were permitted to wash their bodies and heads. The *Apache* stood so closely next to each captive to ensure that would not escape, his breath could be felt upon each as they washed. The *Parussi* were given tall, dry grass to dry their bodies.

This was the system: the captives marched twenty or more miles a day, then stopped by the river to clean and rest for the evening. Food and water was provided to them by the *Apaches* three times per day. Dried fruit, corn kernels, and small pieces of buffalo meat were the only sustenance served. The *Apaches* wanted their bounty to be well-fed and watered upon their arrival in the slave market of Janos.

The captive's cuts and bruises on their feet and hands were treated with *salvia* (aloe vera)—a healing plant. The *Apaches* did not want to arrive with injured commodities of premium trade value. Any swelling was treated with *arnica* (a topical mountain sunflower), crushed into an ointment. The only abrasion that could not be healed were the deep ring cuts skinned into the entire wrists and neck. Those wounds reopened every day of the journey: a reminder of the dreadful forced walk from *Parussi*.

The forced walk took over sixty sunrises. The young *Parussis* knew not where they were going or what their fate would be. Each knew if they took the next step, they might survive. Tied to the aspen lodge-pole, they marched through steep hill mountain valleys, narrow pathways, and over hard mountain dirt ground. Stopping three times a day for water, food, and rest, the *Apaches* were patient to ensure each young captive remained healthy.

Finally, Watili did see her brother Peregrue. He looked at her, always with a dazed look upon his face from the femur clubbing he'd received at their home village. Her brother quietly asked her, "Are you all right?" She answered by nodding her head forward, knowing not to say anything loudly to alarm a nearby *Apache* guard and his waiting buffalo femur hatchet.

The captive group finally arrived at a downward slope of a mountain pass (*La Veta* Pass), and the journey began to ease into a descent. The sloping sides echoed back the sound of a nearby creek and the animal life that surrounded the entire passage. After two days of descent, they arrived at the eastern flat prairie, a place the *Parussi* people had only heard of. This was the flat land where buffalo lived and roamed, a very unique place indeed in Native lore.

A walking *Apache* raiding party approached the group, and the leader of the group knew of them. He rode his horse to meet with them. They greeted each other and laughter could be heard during the conversation. Watili thought to herself: *the raiding party patrolled the entrance to this passage way west towards the mountain; they do not have horses.*

The entire group then turned south on the prairie land of wide open space to the east. Hot and warm spells marked their march. The mountain captives were not used to feeling such spells. They crossed large buffalo swathes crossings and encountered hawks and eagles flying freely above, and thus knew the end of the journey was near.

Finally, they could see a village of adobe buildings in the distance: *Janos*. Little did the group know this town would determine their fate: not the forced march they had endured. They were taken to a *hacienda*. The men were again separated from the women. The Apaches experience had shown them that the emotion of spouses or siblings would arise at the end of the journey. Watili looked at her brother from a distance as they locked eyes of love, thinking each of their parents, perhaps seeing each other for the last time.

Watili wrists and neck were finally unshackled. Deep circular cuts would forever provide the jewelry of her history. In one of the rooms was a bath house where the women were permitted to bathe and clean themselves, comb their hair, and rest for an entire week. The *hacienda* was well-patrolled, and thin timber fences encircled the homes to make sure the slaves would not run. They were given clean white one piece *traje* (dresses) to wear and leather strapped sandals: this clothing the sign of a slave women. Free Spanish women wore dark or black colors and dark leather shoes, quite the contrast.

At the *hacienda*, Watili heard something that pained her head, a language she had never heard before: Spanish. She could tell this language was not from this land. She said to herself: *this language is too complicated: so many words to describe something or to complete a story. I hope I do not have to learn this complexity.* She also saw something she had never seen: a round spoked circle connected to flat cut tree pieces (a wagon). A long-legged horse is tied to this creation, and pulls the cut trees as the spokes revolve in a circle. She saw metal pans, iron shovels, and picks. The sounds of a blacksmith interrupted the calm of the morning, the clang and ring of heavy metal clanging against other metal. The sounds hurt her ears. She didn't understand these new people or their technology.

Finally, the leader of the *Apaches* entered the quarters of the women slaves. Incredibly, he spoke a limited amount of *Ute* the women could understand. The evening meal was *papas* (potatoes), *frijoles* (beans), and *chíle verde* (green chíle) with cow beef slivers. It was like nothing Watili had ever eaten, but she would now understand it was a staple food in this land. The leader begins to tell them they were to be domestic servants in Spanish and Mexican homes, with the opportunity to become Spanish citizens in the near future—if they behaved themselves.

The next morning, the well-rested women were loaded into a wagon and taken to the auction trade house. All were very quiet and nervous during this three-hour ride. They were scared, some holding hands with each other. They only knew that if they ran or fled, harm would await them.

The wagon waited its turn, and then stopped near the front of the plaza. The women got down and stood in line. Slowly, one-by-one, they were marched the front of the plaza to stand upon a makeshift platform stand to be bid upon. All she heard now was the language of money, Spanish, and she realized this tongue is how trade was completed here. Watili, the now-to-be domestic servant, received a premium value of $200. She walked off the platform and out of the plaza entrance to stand alongside the other recently purchased natives.

At the other end of the plaza, she saw someone familiar. Her brother: also looking fit and well-fed. He was marched to the front of the plaza. She noticed his value was much less: $100, for he was destined to work in the silver mine northeast of *Janos*. Watili was excited to see him. She said nothing, then wondered if she would ever see him again.

The *Apache-Mescalero* group leader watched, all smiles, for he knew he received premium pay for a few months of work. He received Spanish *pesetas* for his labor and would immediately exchange them for a highly sought-after horse. He was considered a "good Indian" who posed no risk to the Spaniards or Mexicans. Greed has a way of making traders short-sighted, as this new animal on the prairie would provide the technology natives needed to extend their reign over the prairie lands. They'd be capable of pursuing the buffalo on horseback, not by foot.

Watili was pulled aside and taken into a quiet room of the *hacienda*. There she met her master and mistress, who preferred to be called Father and Mother. They smiled genuinely at Watili and possessed a warm ambiance that made her feel comfortable and safe.

The man said, "*Yo soy el padre*—I am the father." The women stood up and said, "*Yo soy la madre*." Watili figured out she would be taken with them at this point. Watili stood strong and placed her closed palm to her heart and said, "Watili". With that motion, Watili was to keep her name, while most of the other young slave women were given Christian names.

The father opened the door, the mother held Watili by the hand, and they walked out to an awaiting horse buggy. The father sat alone in front and guided the horse, as the two women sat in the back. The mother grinned and felt she had met a new and trusted friend when looking into the kind face of the responsible slave girl.

They rode for over two hours before arriving at a large, well-kept *hacienda* that impressed Watili. The father pulled the horse's reigns to stop and then, suddenly, three small children dashed out the door, "*Mama y Papa!*" they yelled as they jumped into the buggy and the arms of the mother. Watili, at age fourteen, understood now she would assist this father and mother as their domestic servant.

Watili's kind heart and relationship with the children made her a valuable commodity to this family. The father recognized her natural skills and work ethic, and began bringing in a tutor to teach Watili to read, write, and pronounce Spanish words properly. He felt this would greatly benefit the children, since she spent so much time with them. The father bragged about his great decision to bring in slave help, and how he managed to turn this slave girl into a valued asset for his family. Yet he really knew nothing of Watili or her history. Watili knew she had left behind her Oneness with Nature, yet she felt lucky to be in a safe environment, despite never seeing her brother Peregrue again after the auction day.

Watili the Slave Maid

Watili was from the *Parussi* Band: a *Ute* sub-band who lived in present-day northwestern *Colorado* near Meeker. They had prospered in the area since 1500 B.C., maintaining much of the same life values as their forefathers had until the initial entry of the first Europeans and the Dominguez-Escalante expedition of 1776. The *Parussi* Band followed a lifestyle and religion based on the Oneness of Nature and Healing. They were Polytheist, believing in nature gods who controlled weather, rain, animals, and people. Their main god was *Senawah*, the creator of land, animals, food, medicinal plants, and the *Utes* themselves.

Living at a high-altitude in the mountains, the *Parussi* dressed against the cold in long-sleeved shirts and pants made of rabbit or hare fur, and ankle-high moccasins with leather soles of deer skin. They lived in the easily mobile *chozas*. Their diet consisted of herbs, wild berries, piñon nuts, and small game, as well as deer and elk.

The forced march across mountain passes from *Parussi* to El Paso encompasses over 750 miles on foot. Such a journey left light scars on Watili's young body and feet. The farther from home the *Apaches* took her, the more easily she lost her way, despite having explored the area extensively with her medicine-man grandfather while helping him search for the plants and roots he used in his cures.

Among the Natives in the territories, slavery had been a fact of life for hundreds of years. Slave-trade centers existed in *Janos* (northern *Mexico*), and the villages of *Santa Fe* and *Taos* held trade fairs every year in the early spring and fall. The introduction of horses allowed for the ability to quickly travel longer distances, as well as successfully attack smaller bands. In this way, slave-hunting became much easier.

The Spanish newcomers participated in this slave trade, employing many of the abducted natives, the young men particularly, as workers in dangerous mines and as ranch hands. Young women often became domestic servants. Spanish and Mexican families purchased young slave girls, adopted them into the family, and allowed them to live within the same quarters as the family. The females became maids, helping clean the homes or ranches, and assisting in raising the children. The males, as ranch hands, worked either on the ranches, in sawmills, or on dairy farms. Upon reaching their twenty-first birthdays, the youths were emancipated. They were given the opportunity to leave and return to the *Parussi*, or accept their new identities and the right to build a life for themselves as private land owners. Most chose to remain Spanish or Mexican citizens, and enjoyed that privilege. By this method, the monarchy of Spain expanded their empire, and the Church added new Christian members to its family.

The Spanish outlawed slavery in the Americas starting with the *Valladolid Debate*, (1550–1551) the first moral debate in European history to discuss the rights and treatment of colonized people. Bartholomew de las Cases argued that the atrocities committed by colonizers were morally wrong. He claimed Natives were fully human, possessed of God-given souls, and forcefully subjugating them was unjustified. The Spanish used the *Encomiendo* System: the Spanish Crown granted an *encomendero* (individual) the right to exact territory tribute from the Natives in gold, in kind, or in labor to protect them and instruct them in the Christian faith. This permitted colonizers to extract free labor from the native slaves they acquired. This led to the New Laws of Good Treatment and Preservation of the Indians (1524) which prevented the use of the *Encomiendo* system. However, this latter law was generally ignored by the Spanish colonizers in the New World, New Spain, and the colonized territory north of the isthmus of Panama.

In the year 1775, people were categorized based on their ancestry. Different terms were used to define not just people of Native, Spanish, and African heritage, but also their mixed-heritage offspring. For example, a *castizo* was the child of pure-blooded Spanish parents. The child of a Spanish person and a Native was called a *mestizo*. A *mulato* was the offspring of a European and an African.

Watili was categorized as an *esclavo* (a slave) or un *peones* (a peon). As a slave maid, she wore a simple, white, one-piece *traje* (dress) belted about the waist with a leather string. Because of the torrid weather, the dress had no neck-line and was short-sleeved.

Watili had beautiful brown skin with a natural healthy sheen of moisture on her face and arms. She wore her medium-length black hair in a French braid, tied at the bottom with leather strings. With her hair kept up this way, the scars on her neck and wrists were clearly visible: the awful jewelry of slavery that marked her as a survivor of the forced march.

Yet with all this distress in her young life, her gentle and loving nature still shone in her eyes. Her love of life was eternally linked to her memories of her bountiful youth and thoughts of her family: this is how she maintained her sanity. Watili missed her father, mother, and siblings very much. She never knew what befell her brother. She was not permitted to speak her *Ute* language, or feel what it was like to be a child of Nature. She was labeled *un esclavo* (a slave), and this title chained her as domestic help. She could not speak with other natives, for the Spanish feared collusion would lead to a revolt. Yes, she knew many of the other young *Ute* women slaves had been violated by their fathers, and forced to live in the same home with the wife of the father. Some were impregnated and sent away, only to return without the child.

All of this fear and uncertainty created loneliness within her soul; her youth and freedom had been foregone. After all, every form of refuge has its price.

Yet, with all of this fortunate security, Watili lived with fear. The white cloths she wore made her feel empty, like a ghost. She'd been separated from her family, removed from Nature, and she did not know if she would return to *Parussi*: the rock of which she identified. At any time, she knew her security could be removed—she lived in fear of being harmed both physically and mentally.

The Spanish family who adopted her relished this love-of-life she possessed. They granted her freedom to roam in the area around the *hacienda*, permitted friends of her age to visit with her, and taught her the ways of the Spanish. Yet, she knew she was captive; she knew she was owned. She waited for a decision to be made on her future by someone else.

When the mother of the children became ill with small pox and quarantined, Watili stepped in and became the primary care giver, providing *cariño* (care and responsibility) like that of a mother. The father recognized the natural leadership skills Watili possessed and respected her for her abilities as a person, not a slave. She was never treated as a concubine.

Watili was required to attend Mass with the family every Sunday and to be educated in the Catholic faith. This was the way Spanish and Mexican families would "adapt" a Native slave to "civilization" and make that child a Christian. Yet Watili did not forget her One-ness with Nature. After her chores were complete, she would go for long walks and observe the landscape of the dry and hot land where she now lived. This was nothing like the green forests, cool rivers, and abundant wild animals of her *Parussi* past. Then, she would sit and pray with Nature, as she had been taught as a young girl: this Oneness created by the Creator.

Watili Discovers the *Dominguez-Escalante* Trail Map and Journal

Don Bernardo's full name was Don Bernardo Miera y Pacheco. Originally from the town of *Burgos* in northern Spain, he was the son of a Spanish *Cantabrian* Cavalry officer, and had been trained to become a military engineer. A true entrepreneur, he was mostly known as a cartographer. In his early adulthood, he'd served in five military campaigns in New Spain and created detailed maps of many of the expeditions in which he'd traveled. He'd also worked as a geologist, metallurgist, and a *Santero* (a carver of wooden religious images).

Don Bernardo operated numerous businesses in his life, working as a geologist for the mines in the area. He'd decided his office was in need of cleaning. He asked another business man, a close friend who was the father of one of his slaves, to clean his office, which was full of maps due to his secondary occupation as a cartographer. The father, for it was none other than he, volunteered Watili's help, for he knew how responsible and honest she was.

On the day appointed, Watili arrived early to clean the office. She was in awe of the knowledge-filled room whose walls were papered with maps and drawings of expeditions, mining developments, and colored drawings of gold-ore veins and silver-ore veins: all reflected the travels of a learned man. Carving wooden saints was one Don

Bernarado's favorite past-times. His statues of Saint Juan, Mary, and Our Lady of Guadalupe adorned the shelves of his office. A permanent fixture in the room, the one of which Don Bernardo was most proud, was a cartographic table of a drawing from the first expedition through the Rocky Mountains in search of a western passage to the Pacific Ocean. It was the famous *Dominguez-Escalante* Expedition map, traveled by Don Bernardo himself.

Watili glanced at the map as she began to sweep, and something on the map caught her eye. The map had latitude marks on the edges, symbols for mining locations: thick, wiggly lines to show rivers and thin ones for mountain passes. A compass rose in one corner determined true north. She looked closely at the map and noticed the familiar pathway corridor trail she and other slaves had been forced to march, an overpass through the mountains. She could not understand how this map could be drawn or described with such detail. She leaned closer to the old paper, her eyes following the river-line and the mountains to a familiar point in the land: the *Parussi* Band Village of her people, where she'd been captured. Fierce homesickness overcame her heart as she stared in near-disbelief.

Could this be my way home? she wondered, not believing her eyes.

She looked up. Sitting all alone on a shelf was a leather journal. Watili knew that as a slave girl, looking in places that weren't her business could cost her a whipping—or possibly her life. She glanced at the front door and heard nothing; she began slowly opening the first few pages of the rough journal. She began reading, slowly realizing it linked to the map. She understood the journal was recounting the journey, and she saw that the Don had renamed every river, stream, valley, and mountain range. These were not the names her grandfather had told her: the ancient, powerful names her ancestors had given to the detailed topography. She noticed every band name along the journey. Their location on the map had been recorded:

what they looked like and what they wore, ate, their spoken language, and if they were friendly to this expedition.

Don Bernardo had renamed every item he saw with the names of the Christians believers. All of these locations previously had Native names. She thought to herself: *how can he discover something that already has names from the band that lived upon that land?*

Slowly, the door began to open. Watili started, hurriedly shoved the journal back on the shelf, and began cleaning the office.

Don Bernardo entered. "*Buenas tardes*—good afternoon. How is the work going?" he did not glance a second time at the little slave girl, and the glance he had taken was far from detailed.

Coolly, Watili answered, "*Muy bien, Señor*—very good, sir."

She worked for another hour, shyly and quietly. Finally, she said to him, "I will be back in one week, as you requested."

Watili slipped out into the courtyard, still very mystified and shocked to have found a map with her village on it. She thought to herself: *I must tell my brother this!* She had not seen or heard from her brother for two years now, since they were separated at the slave fair in *Janos*, yet her concern and love did not subside.

It was during her third cleaning of Don Bernardo's office that Watili showed her fortitude. He was writing at his desk when she "cowboyed up", firmly standing next to the cartographic table. With a firm forefinger, she pointed to a location on the map and said, "*Yo soy de esto Rancheria*—I am from this village."

Don Bernardo looked up from his writing, and his brows crinkled a little above his nose-bridge as he recognized in his mind what this slave maid had just said: *yo soy de esto Rancherla*. He lifted his head and with his bright blue eyes he intently studied Watili. Only then did he notice the light-colored scars around her neck and wrists. He thought to himself: *she journeyed the passage*.

Don Bernardo slowly got up and walked around his desk. Watili began to tremble, not knowing if he would strike her, yell at her, or maybe ask her to leave and never return, but she stood tall and looked straight ahead.

He stood on the other side of the desk and said to her, "*De donde eres? Di me* - where you are from? Tell me."

Watili turned toward the desk and the map, looked down at the yellowing paper for a moment, and then pointed to a mountain location as she said, "*Parussi*".

Don Bernardo followed her finger, remembering the exact location and village. He looked again at her lightened scars, showing clearly across her brown skin and asked, "You were forced to walk this?"

Watili bravely met his eyes and said, "Yes, many of us from my village, like my brother and me."

"How long was the journey?" Don Bernardo asked.

"We counted almost sixty sunrises," she answered, holding up her hands as though counting on her fingers.

Don Bernardo's lips pursed, and his gaze dropped to the floor. He said nothing and walked back to his desk.

Watili completed her work and simply walked out.

Two weeks had passed when Watili arrived to clean the office again; Don Bernardo was sitting at his desk. She walked in and began sweeping and organizing papers. The curious Watili walked by the cartographic table and said, "I understand your map: the numbers reveal when the sun rises, the wiggly lines refer to the waters, and the arrow refers to the top of Earth. Yet, what do these crossed lines mean?"

A stunned Don Bernardo lifted his eyes and removed his glasses. He wondered to himself, *how does this slave girl understand all this?*

He rose from his desk and walked again to the other side of the table and explained. "That means there is a prospect of finding ore."

Watili looked at the map.

"What is ore?" she asked.

Don Bernardo walked over to his drawings of gold and silver veins. "This is what veins of gold and silver look like," he said, tapping a drawing with one long finger. He glanced at her, but it was clear from her face that it meant nothing to Watili, as her band placed no value on ore.

She then stated proudly of her village, "We have much ore."

To the Spaniard Don Bernardo, outside of providing Christianity to the natives, he knew finding ore was the entire purpose of the Spanish Crown. His blue piercing eyes concentrated on the face of Watili, "Where are you from again?"

Watili pointed to the map. "*Parussi*," she said, as she continued cleaning.

Don Bernardo asked, "What does 'much ore' mean?"

"Very high rock with those golden and silver streaks within a mountain," she explained.

Don Bernardo thought to himself: *the Crown will never grant permission to look for ore in these prohibited lands. But if I go independently and locate these veins, they will listen to me and grant me the riches and positions I desire.*

Agreement to Disclose Gold and Silver Veins for Watili's Freedom

As the weeks passed, Don Bernardo befriended Watili, and listened to her stories of her village and of how much she missed her family. Her weekly visits to Don Bernardo's office provided the opportunity for them to get to know one another. Watili discussed the lives of the mountainous-dwelling *Parussi*, like how she worked with her family and friends on chores that benefited the entire community. Yet, it was clear what she missed most was her family.

"I miss my brother, Peregrue. He is here in the *El Paso* area," Watili told him.

"Where is he?" Don Bernardo inquired.

"I do not know. When we arrived, he was separated with the men. Later I learned that the men were taken to work deep in the silver mines. I have not heard anything or seen him since. That's all I know," she said sadly.

Finally, Don Bernardo told her, "I have purchased the right for you to work for me exclusively. You will live in my *hacienda*, and we will have much work for you."

Watili was not pleased. She was very comfortable living with a family, and she did not fully understand how she could be purchased by others and still be safe with another family. "What was I traded for?" Watili asked.

"Two premium mules and some goats," Don Bernardo said slowly, so as not to upset Watili.

"I am happy. I do not want to live with others," she said adamantly, as it dawned on her she truly had no freedom. "Where I live and work, I am treated with respect. I was only to be loaned to you to clean your office, nothing more."

"You will be very safe and comfortable in my home," Don Bernardo explained. He knew the Spanish did not use separate quarters for their slaves, instead having them live within the family.

This was different than in the southern states of the United States, where separate quarters for African slaves was the norm.

"I do not need for you to watch over my children, yet there is plenty to do on the ranch. More importantly, I want to continue to hear about your village," Don Bernardo said to her.

Watili was hesitant and scared. She realized she could run off like other slaves had done, but she risked suffering hideous consequences. She was unmarried, without a man in her life, and felt comfortable in her role as a simple maid. She knew this would change now.

She looked at her wrists again, the light tan scars on the dark skin of her forearms resembled *pulseras* (bracelets): a brand of her slavery. These reminders of her pain and suffering would forever prompt her bravery.

"You want that gold and silver ore!" she blurted out, as she figured out Don Bernardo's plan.

Don Bernardo was startled and alarmed at this forcing of his hand, for he was all too aware of the fact she possessed the insight of the location of rich veins.

"Yes," he said nervously. "I was thinking we could travel to your village and upon showing me the veins, if they are in fact genuine, you could stay with your village and family."

What Don Bernardo offered was considered treason by the Spanish government and the Crown. An expedition to the north must be granted by the King of Spain himself, and the purpose and process must not harm or encroach on the natives who lived in the unexplored mountain areas.

"Where am I to live? What work must I do, and how will I survive?" Watili asked.

"You will live in my hacienda. We have plenty of work to do, and nobody will bother you," he explained.

Watili pondered this and stated emphatically, "If I am mistreated any way in your hacienda, I will share nothing with you. I will run off and deal with those mistreatments."

Don Bernardo nodded in ascent. Then he explained, "It is a long journey to *Parussi*. We will have to take side-roads once we get to the edge of the Northern Spanish frontier at *Ohkay Owingeh*, a *San Juan Pueblo* village."

"How long will it take?" she asked.

"About three to four weeks to *Ohkay Owingeh* and another three weeks to *Parussi*. I am bringing this up now because there is a caravan from *El Paso* we can join that will take us to *Ohkay Owingeh*. It is not an easy journey. We will have to pass the *Jornado de Muerte* (the Journey of Death)," he explained. "It is a passage of about one hundred miles with no water or shade. Many perish on this journey."

It didn't matter what Don Bernardo said; all of Watili thoughts centered on this opportunity to see her family again. She figured the map would show them the way to *Parussi*; she would be able to translate with bands they encountered in *Ute* or sign-language. Showing him the veins he wanted to see so badly could not make matters any different.

"Don Bernardo, I want to know where my brother Peregrue is," Watili demanded. "He was taken to work in the mines."

"Well," Don Bernardo rubbed his jaw thoughtfully. "There are three main mines here in New Spain in the large towns of *Zacatecas, Texco*, and *Guanajuato*. New Spain is the chief supplier of silver to Spain and the rest of the world."

The silver industry relied heavily on native slave labor. This industry monopolized the water, so the native villages surrounding the area were left with little water to exist, incapable of sustaining their populations.

By the year 1800, a little over one million slave laborers survived out of an estimated eleven million utilized for the free labor in this industry at the beginning of the century. Furthermore, the silver mines' dependency on the monopoly of water prohibited the existence of both nearby native villages and of Spanish farming and ranches in the area.

"Can we go there and look for him?" the naïve Watili asked, with a quiver in her voice.

"We would not know where to look and survivors are rare, I must tell you the truth," Don Bernardo said. Don Bernardo knew that if he showed Watili the dangerous pit mines and the wake of devastation done to the environment, a danger her village faced through the establishment of a silver mine, she would not be willing to take him to the veins in *Parussi*.

Tears filled Watili's eyes as she looked down at the wooden floor. She thought to herself: *he speaks of the real destiny of natives. Why should I stay here and risk more?*

"I will go, Don Bernardo. Understand that I want to see my family and will stay with them." Her voice was firm and the large, dark eyes she turned on him seemed to bore into his very soul.

"Understood. That is our agreement. I will get to see the veins of gold and silver you described," Don Bernardo said. No matter the façade he presented to this girl, he understood clearly the devastating and lasting effects a large finding of gold or silver ore would have on the environment and its people. "I will begin preparing for our journey. I was told you can ride a horse?" he asked.

"Yes. You're the one not raised in the wilderness, as you like to call it," Watili confidently responded, with a smile.

Journey to the Northern Outpost Ohkay Owingeh-San Juan Pueblo

Don Bernardo said, "Watili, we are fortunate; I have located a caravan we can travel along with from here in *El Paso* to *Santa Fe*, and then to the most northern post outside of *Taos*."

"What is a caravan?" Watili asked.

"*Tu sabes*—you know, a procession of wagons?" Don Bernardo answered.

"When does the caravan leave?" asked Watili.

"In the next couple of weeks. I need to pack our saddles with dried foods and *carne seca*-dried buffalo meat to last over a month. We will need items to trade on the journey, knifes with steel edges, hatches, beads of clear, red and blue colors, and pieces ores of silver and gold color." Don Bernardo answered.

"Be sure not to tell anyone of this journey." Don Bernardo said steadfastly. "It is not permitted or endorsed by the monarchy or King of Spain," he explained.

"Why does that matter?" Watili asked

"It's prohibited to enter the lands beyond *Taos* without permission from the King himself, and he would only sanction a trip for an expedition with a specific purpose. The primary purpose of expedition I traveled with previously was to locate a western passage to the Pacific Ocean," Don Bernardo explained.

"Did you locate this passage west to the ocean?" Watili asked.

"I wrote in my journal that no clear passage was located." Don Bernardo explained. "The natives in the Northern Frontier have only had rare exposure to the Spanish *vaqueros* (cowboys). The monarchy does not want these areas developed or exposed to any Europeans."

The 750-mile journey to *Ohkay Owingeh* Band-*San Juan Pueblo* (west of *Taos*, New *Mexico*) in the early month of June 1781 was by all accounts a fortunate opportunity. Five years had passed since Don Bernardo first entered the northern wilderness; this journey beyond *Ohkay Owingeh* was explicitly prohibited by the Spanish social and civic authorities. The fortune lied in that year, when the caravan from *Mexico* City was traveling due north to *Ohkay Owingeh-San Juan Pueblo.*

Don Bernardo readied their horses, and both he and Watili joined the trip to the Northern Frontier on their own secret mission.

Watili asked, "You are carrying no fire sticks?" referring to rifles, muskets, or pistols.

"Yes, I thought it would be safe for the both of us to not have firearms. On the *Dominguez-Escalante* Expedition, we had no arms. This way the natives felt safe in approaching us—*arrimar*," Don Bernardo explained.

"My grandfather mentioned this long trail to me. It is lengthy and very hot. He traded for our village and traveled extensively," Watili explained.

This long journey was established first by the Natives (around 1000 b.c.), who called it the *Rio Grande* Indian Train. The trail was a north-south journey used for the commerce of trade by native traders on foot to the cold northern villages of *Colorado* to the *Aztec* empire *Tenochtitan* and other Mesoamerican civilizations. Many native traders stopped at the northern *Chihuahua, Mexico* Regional Trace Center at *Paquamé* (Casa Grandes) to trade their wares. Traveling without horse or wagon over long distances, the native trade parties carried south lighter items such as macaw and parrot feathers: these items were sought after for their spiritual and ceremonial value. Aztec and Mayan traders also sought copper bells, shells, and turquoise that was mined in the *Cerrillos* hills of New *Mexico*, known as Mount *Chalchihuit* (Turquoise Mountain) by the Aztecs.

El Camino Real de Tierra Adentro (The Royal Road of Interior Land)

The Spanish explorer Juan de Oñate's expedition of 1598 made this trail popular and used by Europeans for the first time. The Franciscan Friar's organized caravans, initially brought items every three years to barter. Later, at its height of usage, the caravan traveled once every three months. The caravan consisted of over thirty oxen-drawn four wheel carts that traveled ten to fifteen miles per day with a soldier escort. Many traveled by foot in a searing heat close to 100 degrees, over barren lands, trails of dust, and with the risk Native attacks. The caravan stopped at resting places called *parejas*, spaced ten to fifteen miles apart that had natural water springs and trees with shade.

"We have been traveling a more than a week now. How much longer?" asked Watili.

"Quite a bit more, it is a slow journey, but the safest possible. We are coming up to the half-way point, which is the most dangerous." Don Bernardo explained.

"Dangerous? I see no danger. You fear Indian attacks; I see nothing." Watili observed.

"It is not the Indians that we fear. It is nature. We will turn north shortly; nature will eat you alive here. Many have perished here, more will parish here," Don Bernardo fearfully explained.

Halfway through the journey they came upon the *Jornado de Muerte* Trail, an uninhabited desert basin of sand and mesquite shrubs where no water and shade existed for ninety miles (the trail lies east and crosses *Las Cruses-Socorro*, New *Mexico*). Prior to entering the basin, barrels of water were brought and filled to the brim to use on the risky endeavor. Deep arroyos, canyons, quick sand, extreme heat, and hardship permitted only eight to ten miles of travel per day. The caravan traveled day and night to get through this stretch, yet many oxen, horses, and pack donkeys could not withstand the fatigue and perished.

The caravan brought red chili pepper, apples, cattle, oxen mules, sheep, goats, chickens and ducks, and cats and dogs. This influenced tribal life with commodities never seen before in the isolated north. This convoy would forever change the landscape of the people and the land; for the first time the natives would not be dependent on the Oneness with Nature to provide sustenance for life.

Yet, what brought the most substantial change in Native values and customs was the introduction for the first time of an organized religion into existing fixed-structure bands along the *Rio Grande* River system (and also to rural bands away from the river system). To receive or trade the new commodities that made life easier to survive, such as the cows or sheep, participation in the new Christian Catholic religion was required. Gathering for Masses and school programs for native youth directed by the friars, changed the Oneness between the natives and Nature. The dependency relationship between Nature and the natives would be lost forever. The natives would no longer solely depend on the rainfall that determines herb, berry, and piñon counts each year; the direction of the buffalo passage; a drought that would force them to move to a new location. Now the Christian God, networking, communication, planning of crops, and breeding of herds would determine the next year's existence.

After three weeks, the caravan arrived in the city of Santa Fe. They were never threatened by Native raids. It was a safe journey for all.

Don Bernardo and Watili rested a few days and re-supplied before their trip north, following the *Rio Grande* river to *Ohkay Owingeh-San Juan Pueblo* Village (near Taos, New *Mexico*), a distance of three hundred and fifty miles. Passing ancient Pueblo bands with the separate languages of *Piro, Towa Keres, Tiwa,* and *Zuni*, Watili was surprised to see such large Native adobe villages at each rest stop. The last leg of the caravan trip carried less oxen carts: about fifteen of them.

On the return trip back to *Mexico* City, the caravan carried textiles of woven wood, tan hides of buffalo, and deer and beaver pelts. Dry meat buffalo and deer were also in demand. Precious metals such as turquoise, peridot, serpentine, and garnet made the journey south along with pottery, clay, salt, and alibati flints. This cycle provided the beginning of the Spanish development and entrance into the American Southwest.

Upon arriving in *Ohkay Owingeh-San Juan Pueblo* Village, Don Bernardo camped near ancient hot springs (present-day *Ojo Caliente*), and then quietly walked off and bathed in the healing waters as Watili oversaw the camp. She wondered where he had run off to.

Don Bernardo returned refreshed from his time at the hot springs, holding in his hands a pouch.

"What did you bring back from the hot waters?" Watili asked.

Don Bernardo handed over the pouch to her. She pulled open the leather strings and saw a glimmering rock. "What is this? I've never seen this shine before?" Watili asked.

"Mica flat flint rock: it's shiny and glitters in the sun." Don Bernardo answered, "We will use this to trade with the natives up north."

"How did you know to find this rock in the hot waters?" Watili asked.

"We all have our secret veins of ore now, don't we, Watili?" He smiled and rolled out his bedding, then quickly fell asleep.

Gold Dust in *Wayatola* [Wa-ha-toy-a] (Mountain Breasts of Earth)

Watili and Don Bernardo awoke long before sunrise, so as not to alert anyone of their impending forbidden journey. Travelling on horseback, they first wandered through wooded mountains and then to the open plains of the beautiful *San Luis* Valley, home to the *Capote* Band. Don Bernardo had passed this valley previously, pressing as closely to the eastern ridge of two mountain ranges to avoid bothering any of the natives in his way. The journey was a two-day horse ride to the summit of *La Veta* Pass: opening east to prairie land.

Watili rode with Don Bernardo, uncomprehending that this journey was treasonous in the eyes of the civic authorities. The journey was quiet as Don Bernardo intended, and finally on the afternoon of the second day they stopped to camp at the mouth of the pass. There they dismounted and stood, amazed by the eastern view of the lower mountain ridges, frosted with unthawed snow peaks. Beyond them lay the sight of flat eastern plains that promised warmer climates. To the unknowing, the Eastern Plains were little more than a beautiful view, but to the learned: this eastern passage provided the warmer weather and the buffaloes' red meat mountain Natives cherished. Once, the buffalo had also been creatures of the mountains, but they'd been driven into the flat plains by hunters, never to return to higher altitudes.

Watili said, "I recognize this passage downward, but we came from the other side of the mountain range."

"Isn't this land beautiful, with its untouched towering mountain peaks and meadows as far as the eye can see? The air: smell it!" said Don Bernardo, as he inhaled the clean, crisp mountain air.

"I wouldn't know. My band and I were in such pain, we didn't bother to look up and see the beauty," Watili scoffed at Don Bernardo under her breath. Waltili had gained confidence in speaking directly back to Don Bernardo as they entered the native and free lands she was accustomed to living within. They made camp that night and were asleep by early nightfall, tired from a long two-day ride.

The *Huajojatola* (Hua-wa-toy-a) Mountains (present-day Spanish Peaks in Walsenburg, *Colorado*) was Don Bernardo's final destination on this part of the trip. He had been to this clandestine location on previous occasions. There were risks on this leg of the journey, he knew, as *Apaches* patrolled this pass to bar entrance to other Native bands, as well as the Spanish from the eastern plains. There had been skirmishes in the area between Spanish and *Apaches*; the *Apaches* did not run and hide at the sight of a horse or a musket, and they did not fear the new *vaqueros*. The brave *Apache* would fight in small bands with effective strategies. They were fervent protectors of their land, best described as nationalistic in a way: the Indian way. The Spanish adopted the *Apache* name from the *Tewa* natives, who called them *Apahu* (stranger or traitor). The first Europeans to see this buffalo-hunting *Apache* Tribe were the 1540 *Coronado de Vasquez* Expedition; they named the natives they had seen the *Querecho*.

In the morning, Don Bernardo and Watili remounted their horses and began the trek downward. By nightfall, they camped on the banks of the *Cuchara* River at the foot of the *Huajojatola* Mountains.

They made camp and slept comfortably in the warmer foothills of the prairies to the east. Watili was glad to be out of the mountain cold she'd lived in for so many years.

Don Bernardo woke early and started a small fire to warm the *atole*. He contemplated not taking Watili to his final stop, instead leaving her at the top of the pass, but he was concerned by the possibility she could be captured by a Capote or one of the other scouting groups he knew patrolled the area.

Don Bernardo and Watili quickly broke camp, and began following an obscure and scarcely traveled path west toward the Eastern Spanish Peak. Then they followed *Wahatoya* Creek until they came to the mouth, which broke off, traversing the mountain with no clear pathway. Finally, Don Bernardo pulled on the reins and stopped.

"*Aqui llegamos*—we've arrived," he said, and both dismounted.

Watili thought she could hear a stone-grinding friction from inside the mountain. She followed Don Bernardo as he slid between two flatiron rocks and entered a cavern. Inside they both stopped; within this cavern existed a discreet mining operation run by three men whose donkeys ground constantly at a chisel. A natural water spout cleansed the rock and washed up the mighty gold.

The three men looked up and saw Don Bernardo and his companion.

One said, "Don Bernardo! *Como estas, joven*—how are you, young man? We knew you were planning to visit. Still, what a surprise!"

Don Bernardo answered, "Yes, a short visit. I am on a scouting expedition for more ore, maybe much more than you have here."

A tall man with broad shoulders and narrow hips, whose muscles bulged beneath his thick cotton shirt, strode forward and reached for Don Bernardo's hand, pumping it with gusto. This was Miguel. Miguel said, "Really? In what parts?"

"This is why I brought this *India*; her name is Watili. She claims to know where the *Ute* Tribe have their veins of gold and silver and knows of their mining techniques," said Don Bernardo.

"*De verdas*—the truth?" said Miguel. "Nobody has found those."

"I have come by for some gold dust I want to use on some of my *santero* carvings. Do you have any extra dust?"

Don Bernardo was a *santero*: a master craftsman of the softwood carved and painted religious art of standing saint figures. This he'd learned from his father, a pedigree *santero* artist. Unique to Don Bernardo's carvings was the final sprinkling of gold dust upon the feet or shoulders of the statue to provide regal lineage of his Christian works of art. He risked much and traveled far to gather this exclusive dust to use as a brand for his work. Very few people knew or understood where and how he could obtain such an opulent element to accent his art.

"We do. Here, grab a pouch and take some. We just scraped this up yesterday," Miguel said.

Don Bernardo grabbed a few pouches, filled them to the brim, and tied them off with the leather ties.

Miguel asked, "Did you see any trace of *Apaches* outside? *Los Querechos*?" referring to the original name the Spanish gave the *Apaches*.

"I have not. Their patrols are very discrete, you know? I do not want to make a scene, and we must go now so we don't disclose any of your operations," Don Bernardo said, shaking hands with his old friend.

"*Si, entiendo*—yes, I understand," said Miguel. "When will we see you again?"

"*No se*—not sure. I am living in *El Paso*. Come look me up when you go to market with your precious gems."

"*Esta bien*—all is good," said Miguel, and he watched the two quickly depart.

Don Bernardo and Watili mounted their horses. It was early afternoon when they headed down the mountain, hoping to be at a level and warm place before nightfall. As they traversed the mountain, following the creek to their camp site, they heard an unusual moan coming from the *Cucharas* River.

The Injured Cibolero

The horse stood more than sixteen hands high at his withers, a beautiful gray stallion with a thick chest and mane, strongly built and very docile. Its regal appearance told Don Bernardo a lot about its master, this injured *Cibolero* (Spanish Buffalo Hunter). As he drew closer to the horse, he saw this was an *Andalusa* (Andalusian breed)—from Old Iberia.

Don Bernardo thought to himself: *this breed is not very common in this country.* He grabbed the reins quietly so as not to spook the horse; it only shifted its hooves a little and kept looking down at its master, who was lying on the ground and moaning.

Glancing around, Don Bernardo saw something he had not seen for many years: a broken *vara* (lance) that led him to believe this man was a *rejonero* (bull fighter) who had fought a bull on horseback in the exquisite bull rings in Madrid and Barcelona.

This thought caused him to look closely at the horse's saddle, a 16th century Spanish saddle made of quality rawhide leather with a high pommel and cantle made of carved wood; the thick flaps had an interesting design: a red stained six-point pomegranate-sepal he recognized from his old country of Spain.

Looking down from her horse, Watili quickly scrutinized the injured man lying on his back on the riverbank. The most obvious injury came from a broken arrow, lodged just below his right clavicle. He had been bleeding for some time, and the shaft was soaked with blood.

"This man is badly injured," she said in shock. She knew she had to remove the arrowhead and shaft to stop the bleeding or this man would die.

She quickly dismounted, and pulled the man from the riverbank onto grassy, flat, dry ground. She grabbed at the long reeds growing along the embankment, yanking them out by the roots to make a *choza*. As a child in her *Parussi* village, she had learned how to make these open-topped reed huts, and she had not forgotten these skills even while living with the Spanish family.

Watili's voice rose to a high pitch. "*Por favor*—please! Get me dry firewood and *ocote* (fire starter)!" she told Don Bernardo, as she quickly hurried to the river. There, she grabbed handfuls of cotton balls and white, mature cotton hanging down from the trees adjacent to the river.

Don Bernardo returned with armfuls of dry wood and *ocote*. Watili asked another thing of him: "Please, let me have dry linens from your saddle!"

They built a small *choza* around the stranger, with a wood fire warming the interior.

Her first diagnosis was that the shaft of the arrow was made of hard mesquite wood. This wood was only available in southern New Mexico where the *Apaches* lived, and she recognized this wood would hold firm when she attempted to remove the arrow. She also noticed the thick tree-bark gel that held the arrowhead to the shaft. She looked closely for white fluids or bubbling of the skin surrounding the puncture: this would mean that the arrowhead had been dipped in poison. Poisons come in various strains from plants, venomous snakes, or the petrified flesh of a dead animal. The petrified flesh was especially difficult to remove because it bred worms that feasted on the torn flesh and grew around the wound. Luckily, everything looked clean.

Don Bernardo watched in amazement as Watili deftly handled the injured man. She turned toward him as she unbuttoned *Cibolero's* long-sleeved cotton shirt. "May I borrow your metal knife?" she asked, removing the shirt from the ailing man's body.

By now, the *choza* was warm from the fire with only Watili and the stranger in the hut. There was no alcohol or any way to relieve the pain of the wound. Don Bernardo peered in from outside the reeds as he brought more dry wood to heat the make-shift house.

Later, Watili called for him.

"Come in, Don Bernardo," she said. "It is time to remove this shaft. You will need to hold him down." She thought to herself: *it would have been nice if the Apaches left mescal cactus to numb the pain*: referring to the fact that the numbing plant was available to the *Apache Mescaleros* in southern New *Mexico*.

As Don Bernardo entered, she instructed him to sit astride the stranger's chest, legs crossed over the waist, and use his hands to pin the healthy shoulder to the ground.

Watili disinfected the knife by holding the blade over an open flame. Letting it cool a bit, she proceeded to cut diagonally into the wound, opening the circumference wider. The stranger moaned in agony. Watili inhaled sharply, then poked her right index finger into the hole and felt around for the arrowhead. She used her finger as a hook to push the arrowhead down, clear of muscle and veins. Then, gently twisting—she unseated the arrowhead, gripped it firmly, and yanked upward, pushing her left hand against the man's chest for leverage. The arrowhead broke free with a force that surprised both Watili and Don Bernardo.

Blood began to spout out of the enlarged hole. Watili grabbed the cotton balls and used them to suppress and soak up the blood. Don Bernardo could barely hold the man down as his legs and healthy arm flailed in all directions.

Watili began to murmur soothingly., "Shhh, shhh, shhh." The stranger opened his eyes. Upon realizing the arrow shaft had been removed, he calmed down. Watili gathered the blood-soaked cotton balls and tossed them into the fire, then applied new cotton balls to the open wound, never letting the blood dry into an uncomfortable scab. She did this for over two hours; little by little the blood flow began to diminish. Finally, she used the cotton balls to fill the length of the wound, and then used the white linens to firmly wrap the injured shoulder.

The *Cibolero* was unconscious now, and running a high temperature from the massive blood loss. Watili asked Don Bernardo to watch him as she went to her saddle and obtained some strange leaves, fresh water, and her cups. She re-entered the *choza* with a pouch, and knelt to pray beside the man.

Don Bernardo just looked at her in amazement. "Where did you learn this?" he asked.

Watili just kept praying and Don Bernardo left the *choza*.

After stabilized the *cibolero*, and calming her own nerves, she took to studying this odd person. His hair was curly, thick, long, and of a shade she had never seen. It was a deep red color: the same color her grandmother had created when dying a blanket or choosing a dye for a skin markings or a clay pot. Never had she guessed this shade of hair could exist.

She placed a clean pan of river-water to slowly boil over the fire and placed *yerba buena* (mint leaves) in the water. She then found a flat log, wiped it clean, and pulled from her pouch some roots she called Bear Root or Osha Root, and proceeded to chop this root into a powder with the fascinating metal knife.

Watili stared at the stranger; his eyes began to twitch and the heat within the *choza* had caused him to sweat. Droplets of moisture beaded on his forehead and upper lip. She knew this was the tipping point: if the fever did not break, the stranger would not live through the night. She glanced again at his unique curly, red locks—wet with the sweat of healing, she hoped.

Watili changed the bandage, removing the linen cloth and the reddened cotton balls. She tossed these into the fire, then blew her warm breath onto the wound, and saw that the flow of blood had firmed within the diagonal cut. With her finger, she gently spread the Bear Root powder upon the wound and cut in half some more cotton balls, placing the flat faces across the wound. To hold the wound firm, she rebandaged it with more linen cloth, all the while continuing her prayer.

At that moment, the stranger opened his eyes. Groggy and only semi-conscious, he was surprised to see the beauty of Watili. He glanced at his shoulder, and did not see the shaft of the arrow in his chest; surprisingly, he had little pain. He looked at Watili with appreciation and gently smiled at her.

Watili was happy to see him regain consciousness. She turned and removed the pan of boiling water from the fire, now tea-colored from the *yerba buena*. She poured a cup of calming, pain-relieving liquid and blew on the cup to cool it; the stranger watched this act of compassion appreciatively. Slipping a firm but tender brown hand under his neck, she offered the warm tea to the stranger to drink. He began to wonder: *did I wander into a band or village*? He finished sipping the tea and lay back down, warm and relaxed.

The stranger turned his head and asked this young woman of nineteen years of age, "*Eres Cristiana*—are you Christian?"

Watili understood the Spanish question, but did not answer him. Her religion was one of Nature and Healing, something she practiced unselfishly in saving this man's life. Her belief was in the Creator who controlled the weather, rain, animal, people, and harvest.

At that innocent and earnest moment, Don Bernardo poked his head into the *choza* and noticed the stranger with his eyes open.

"Ah!" Don Bernardo said, "*Como estas, Cibolero*—how are you, Buffalo Hunter?" He did not notice that delicate and altruistic warmth of Nature and Healing had been changed with his intrusion.

Cibolero answered, "*Bien*—good," but he did not forget the tender moment that had existed in the *choza*.

"Where am I?" he asked, voice barely audible.

"You are at the foot of the Huajojatola Mountain near the Cuchara River," Don Bernardo answered. "Do not talk. Save your energy, and we will talk in the morning." He could see from this man's weakened state he might not make it through the night, so Don Bernardo removed himself from the warm environment.

Watili felt *Cibolero's* moist forehead, then cleaned his face with a linen cloth. "Shhh, shhh, shhh." She mused as the man fell once again into a comfortable sleep. Watili stayed by his side, praying for his health and his life, and for the chance to see her own family soon.

Throughout the night, she kept the *choza* very warm; every hour she would redress the wound with the Bear Root powder and give the man warm tea when he awoke. After sunrise, the *Cibolero* awoke and tried to sit up by himself. Watili stopped him and asked, "*Tienes hambre*—are you hungry?"

The *Cibolero* nodded his head in the affirmative.

In one of her pouches, she placed a handful of *avena* (oatmeal grain with dry raisins) into the pan of water above the fire. After a few minutes, she poured this thick broth into a cup. Then, placing her arms behind the man's healthy shoulder, she lifted him into a sitting position that permitted him to drink. He finished the *avena*, and he felt strength return to his body.

Don Bernardo heard the noise coming from the *choza*, and entered to see the condition of this man.

"I see you have some strength," he said, looking at the man partially sitting up, propped by the strength of Watili. "Tell me, how did you get here?"

Cibolero spoke softly, remembering. "Myself and two other *vaqueros* decided to go onto the plains to hunt buffalo. We had watched for days from afar before and saw how the *Indios*—"the Indians" pursued the *bisote*—buffalo. When we thought there was no one in the area, we entered the plains in search of *bisote*, but we were surprised by a trap arranged by the Apache. They were waiting for us. I think I was the only one to get away, but was hit by this arrow as I escaped on my horse. My horse! How is he?" *Cibolero* asked worriedly.

"Your horse is fine. Quite an *andalusa*," said Don Bernardo. He looked at Watili. "Watili worked her magic to save your life; I don't know how she came into this knowledge."

"My knowledge comes from my grandfather and mother. He is a medicine man who understands the uses of herbs and prayer to heal," Watili answered.

"Ahhh, I see. Well, let's rest today; I will snare some rabbits for our food, and see how you are feeling this evening. We do not know where that *Apache* raiding party is, so let's lay low." Don Bernardo left the *choza,* and began his hunt for meat.

Cibolero looked at Watili. He greatly appreciated that this women had saved his life. "I want to thank you," he said, sitting up. He drank more of the *yerba buena* tea on his own.

Watili just looked at him, noting how his rumpled red locks curled over and around his ears. Throughout the day, she placed more wood on the fire to ensure his life would be saved by its warmth. *Cibolero* just rested and drank the broth given to him; his fever finally broke.

In the late afternoon, Don Bernardo returned to the camp carrying two rabbits which he quickly skinned, then brought into the *choza* with a big smile on his face.

"Dinner tonight," he said, as he ran a skinny stick through the rabbits and began to slow roast them over the fire.

"Very skillful," said Cibolero with approval. "Used a snare and no noise from your rifle!"

"Watili is not the only one with Indian skills," Don Bernardo said, with a chuckle. "How are you feeling? You look much better."

"Watili has brought life back to me. I was able to stand and go outside this hut earlier today," said Cibolo.

"I think to be safe, we should leave early in the morning. You have trespassed into *Apache* land, and they do not like anyone except their own." Don Bernardo mused. "We can go up this pass on the winding south side: not an easy path, but I think it will be safe. We want to go visit Watili's village."

"I would be interested in seeing that," said *Cibolero*. Watili smiled.

"I have traveled in the area before, with an expedition five years ago. We are going to follow that exact route once we get up to the mountain passes," Don Bernardo explained.

What Don Bernardo neglected to mention to *Cibolero* was that the Spanish government prohibited any visitation to the area without express permission, and this little venture, if discovered, would be punishable as treason.

Little did they know what they would witness that day.

Battle for La Veta Pass

On the third morning of *Cibolero's* rest, he awoke and felt he could travel by horse. Don Bernardo knew the *Apache* raiding party must surely be searching for this wounded Spaniard, yet they did not know the exact location where he fell—traveling by foot, they would not be able to track him with any expediency.

At daybreak, the group arose and tore down the *choza* to leave no trace of their stay. *Cibolero* was able to stand upright. Wearing leather chaps on his legs, a leather *chaleco* (vest) and rawhide boots, he looked very much the *vaquero* who would wrestle the untamed land of New Spain. Leaving behind the river (present-day *Cuchara* River) Don Bernardo helped *Cibolero* mount his gray *Andalusa,* and the three travelers began the trek up the *La Veta* Pass once again. Don Bernardo knew not to follow the normal trail route; instead they clung to the south side of the pass, which was much rockier and abundant in trees and shrubs.

The pathway was rough, and the going was slow. Many times, the travelers dismounted their horses to lead the beasts through the rocky embankments and steep ridges on the unforgiving mountainside. Don Bernardo felt this was necessary as he understood the *Apache* mind-set: they fought for revenge in battle and in retaliation for the disturbance of their sacred land. They'd doggedly pursued the

Cibolero to locate the intruder, the *vaquero*, and they possessed the endurance and brass to keep looking for him.

Cibolero shifted his weight on the Andalusian's back, peering down into the ravine. Suddenly, the movement of *Apache* warriors, the same who had pursued him a few days earlier, caught his eye. He quietly gestured for Don Bernardo and Watili to look downward. Thankfully, the three travelers were hiking through thick forest and brush, and could not be seen from the floor of the pass. Their own high vantage point permitted a clear view of what was about to unfold: the unexpected clash between two rival raiding parties. Never before had any white men seen Natives battle over a territory.

Watili grabbed the reins of all three horses and moved up the mountainside to a flat grading. Don Bernardo and *Cibolero* froze where they stood to watch the storm of combat that was about to take place.

As the two opposing parties recognized one another, the contrast in their attire could not be more different. This was due in part to the mighty buffalo, or *bisonete*, as the Spanish called the beast.

The *Onellos*, a *Caputa* Band, were from the high, broad mountain valleys near present-day *San Luis, Colorado*. In the year 1775, the North American continent was experiencing a mini-ice age. George Washington and his Continental Army suffered extremely bitter cold as they fought the British. The elders of the *Onellos* Band also felt this cold spell, and sent these twelve warriors (in the early spring month of April) on an exploratory mission to gauge the possibility of moving their high-altitude camp either into the lower part of the *La Veta* Pass or onto the flatter, much warmer prairie that was patrolled by *Apache* raiding expeditions.

The *Onellos* expedition wore thin, long-sleeved shirts made of rabbit or hare hide. The warriors were slender with light complexions, as befit their mountain lifestyle. Tied to their backs were quivers made of hare-skin that held eight to ten arrows; the arrowheads were shaped from flint rock, and the fletching was cut from turkey feathers. The curved bows of hardened mulberry wood utilized hemp for bowstrings. A small, six-inch, flint knife was tied to the waistband of each warrior.

The *Apache-Jicarilla* were of darker complexion, thicker in body mass, and in possession of more strength. Their bodies were well-nourished from the red meat and bone marrow that provided a physical advantage over the lesser-nourished mountain warriors. The *Jicarilla's* winter attire consisted of thick, long-sleeve shirts with thick leggings and buffalo-hide shoes that laced up in front. Over all they wore a thick shawl that tied in front as an exterior coat. Bound to their backs were thick quivers that also held eight to ten arrows. These, unlike the weapons of their enemies, were fletched with goose feathers, and their bow strings were made of high-strength rawhide.

They also carried sharpened hatchets of buffalo femur-bones in their waistbands; these weapons were of a strategic advantage in hand-to-hand battle.

This specific Apache-Jicarilla group had a definite purpose: oppose intruders and guard the wide easy passageway from the high mountains to the plains. Their intent was to prevent the advantages of buffalo meat being shared with competing bands. *La Veta* Pass Summit was above 9,000 in elevation and more than five miles in width. The *Apache-Jicarilla* young forward scouts were physically prepared to scour the lengthy distances and tough mountain terrain to inform the primary party of any intruders coming into the passage way to the east.

Training for young *Apache* warriors began at a young age. Coming from a nomadic band that moved often, young boys were required to carry heavy loads as they moved from one region to another region—practice for properly positioning themselves in a buffalo hunt.

As a way of expanding lung capacity, establishing extended endurance in battle, or training for lengths of time when they would not be part of the main village, young boys had to run long distances or up mountain trails with water in their mouths to force them to breathe through their noses. They were also sent on short-distance hunting expeditions without rations as a way to practice hunting rabbits, hares, rats, snakes, or any other small game with their bows and arrows. They would have no food to eat other than what they killed, and thus they were taught to survive.

As the two opposing warrior groups sized each other up and squared off, both spread into an aligned formation behind small trees, boulders, and crevices in mountain terrain. Both parties knew this was to be a conflict for survival, driven by the desire to access the buffalo and all the advantages the animals provided. The Onellos spoke the historic *Ute* language of *Yutas*, while the *Apache* spoke the Eastern *Apache* dialect known as *Athabaskan-Na Dene*. Normally, these two long-time enemy groups were separated by one mountain range and would not be able to communicate with one another; but for the conflict today, communication was not necessary.

The experienced *Apache-Jicarilla* warriors fought all their battles with a strategy in mind. In this case, they fought in pairs. The first warrior's objective was to force his opponent into divulging their defensive position in order for the second warrior to have a clean shot with their arrow. Successfully striking down an opponent prevented the necessity of resorting to hand-to-hand combat. The *Apache* strategy was simple, yet with valor: standing behind a natural barrier such as a slender tree or rock, the first warrior grunted and hurled rocks at their opponent to scare or force him out. When this did not work, the brave *Apache* warrior would expose himself on one side for a fleeting moment, and then scurry back under cover as the second warrior would rise up with bow—his arrow ready to be unleashed.

In a second skirmish, the *Apache* pair would quickly build a stone wall of smaller rocks up to three or four feet in height and six feet in width. This defensive fortification was called *refugios* (refugees) by the Spanish militia who opposed these warriors. The Spanish felt this skilled strategy of defense was extraordinary difficult to assault. From behind this *refugio*, the *Apache* warriors would throw smaller rocks and anticipate when the *Onillos* would advance. Then they would rise up, using the stone wall to shield their bodies, and release an arrow at the advancing mountain warrior.

It did not take long for the *Apaches* to wound, maim, and kill all of the *Onellos*. The killing of the entire party was rooted in some ancient reason, possibly a prior battle with the *Onellos* in which a blood relative or friend was lost. *Apaches* feared the dead or the spirit of the dead: an odd thing, considering how they were able to kill without remorse.

The white femur hatchets were covered in red blood and green stains. The *Apaches* took no scalps, for this was not their historic custom. Only the regal *Onello* bows and arrows, their flint knives, and any excess food of seeds and berries were carried off. The bodies of the mountain residents were left for Mother Earth to consume.

After the victory, the *Apache* warriors did not celebrate. There was no joy in them, only the calm that came with the knowledge their rhythm of life with Nature would continue for another day. In this abrupt and heated battle, the pursuit of the *Cibolero* was all but forgotten.

As tacticians themselves, Don Bernardo and *Cibolero* were stunned at the strategy and efficiency of the *Apache* warriors. The two men stared at each other with mutual wonderment. Quietly, they both glanced behind themselves to find Watili, who had known the outcome of the battle before it began. The three stealthily climbed up the embankment and grabbed the reins of the horses before quietly walked west up the pass, away from the overview of the ravine. All three were stunned at the defensive tactics used by the *Apaches* to protect the sturdy war instruments, the food source provided by the buffalo, and their rights to the advantages of a warmer environment.

The Journey to Watili's Village

The excursion to obtain Gold Dust at Wahatoya created a barrier against the journey to locate the village of Watili. As the group arrived at the top of the passage (present-day Fort Garland, *Colorado*), Don Bernardo traveled by latitude makers: he knew they'd arrived at the 37°: a crossroads between mountain ranges. They had a choice of either turning south and locating the original route of the *Dominguez-Escalante-Dominquez* Map, or going north and perhaps saving three days of travel—and somehow traversing the mountains eastward to locate the original route.

Watili demonstrated her fearlessness of the open mountain country by kicking her horse forward, "We are going south. The *Capote* Band control this area; it would be best if we avoid them," she knew this territory well. They were going south and avoiding the northern trail: the forced walk and possibly the impassable snowy mountain range. They had three to four hours left of daylight left when they arrived at present-day *Alamosa, Colorado*.

As they dismounted and made camp, Don Bernardo marveled at the beauty of the land and the opportunities it offered and said, "We could have saved time by going north."

Watili retorted, "I was forced-walked from my village down that pass (*La Veta*). I have scars on my wrist and neck to prove my journey. We walked and traversed the mountain passes in mid-summer to get to this location at the mouth of this pass. We must go south to avoid the snowy high mountain passes and travel within the ranges on the west side of these mountains to get to my village. "

Cibolero questioned, "Forced-walked? You were enslaved?"

"Yes, the *Apache-Mescaleros* arrived by horseback into our hidden village. We thought they were Spanish slavers at first when we first heard the calamity. It was early morning; my brother and I were sleeping in our parent's *choza*. When we heard the snorting of large animal nostrils and the hoofs beating the ground, we knew there was danger. We had heard of slavers.

"Everyone scattered. The *Apaches* ran us down on their horses and hit us down with clubs. Then those who were captured were gathered together: in all about forty of us." Watili explained. "They wanted only those who were young: those that could handle the march. So my mother and father were left behind at the village.

"Then they cut down a skinny lodge pole and tied our necks and wrists with aspen-back slivers to this pole, maybe six people to a side. Then we started this walk; they would hit us with skinny branches or those clubs if we slowed down or refused to walk. Everyone was crying."

"How long was the march? You were tied to these poles the entire march?" *Cibolero* concernedly asked.

"The journey took about sixty sunrises—sixty days. After we were far away from our village, they told us in their language they would remove the poles—but if we ran, they would run us down and club us. They gave us water and food frequently, they did not violate the women, and they let us bath in river water to keep clean. These *Apaches* also spoke Spanish. I did not recognize even the language; I thought it was maybe another Indian language. Then I learned Spanish in El Paso and realized the *Apaches* spoke Spanish," Watili said.

"Where did they take you?" *Cibolero* asked.

"They took us to a slave-trading center in *Janos* (Near *Chihuahua, Mexico*). The young women were sold to Spanish or Mexican families to work as maids and servants for their families. The men were forced to work grueling forced labor in the silver mines. My brother is still there; I don't know if he is alive or dead."

"Where did you learn to speak Spanish?" *Cibolero* asked.

"The family Don Bernardo bought me from taught me to read and write in Spanish so I could assist their children. I lived within their home and was fortunate to get to be with their family."

"Yes, an opportunity for the Spanish is slavery for others. My brother is still working the mines near Janos, I hope." Watili answered.

"Who enslaved you?" asked *Cibolero*.

"The Apache-Mescaleros from the Southern Territory. I do not know how they found us; we hide very carefully," answered Watili.

Neither Watili nor *Cibolero* realized the map-maker they'd traveled with had provided the route to locate and capture slaves to be sold to market in the Janos-area.

Don Bernardo quickly changed the subject, "Tell me Cibolero, you have a red flower imprinted on your saddle. I recognize that flower, what is it?"

"That is a pomegranate sepal. I just thought it was pretty, it reminds me of home," said *Cibolero*.

"Where is home?" Don Bernardo asked.

"My family is originally from Segovia, Spain, but we have spent much time in New Spain now. I was part of a mobile infantry unit to explore this new territory."

"Were you part of the *Companies Volantes* or mobile or flying companies of the Spanish squadron?" Don Bernardo asked.

The *Compañias Volantes* or mobile or flying companies originated in 1712 as light cavalry units that patrolled the frontier of New Spain. In contrast with the traditional heavy-horse cavalry units and stationary garrison, these cavalry squadrons were designed to provide rapid and quick responses to hostile raiders, and then conduct extended offensive patrols in the areas. They were to carry handguns, rifles, saddles, provisions, and an extra horse to deploy hostiles for more than one day without rest.

"Yes, the high-flying *Compañias Volantes*. We were the first Europeans to ever hunt the beast-cow-*baca*, the buffalo-*bisonete, the big dog*!" *Cibolero* said with excitement. "This we did when we were not on patrol on the eastern *llano*-plains."

"The first Coronado expedition of 1541 were in this area. They told stores of the *Querecho*-an *Apache* Band that followed and hunted these beasts *de pie*-by foot. The formed small bands of hunters; they were very effective."

"It is said the *Querecho* reminded the Coronado expedition of the *Arabé*-Arabs; they used dogs to pull travois, hides, and food; and they also did not have horses. Coronado was also impressed by the endurance of the warriors, who could run after a buffalo an entire day before downing the *bisonete*."

"Did you learn much from their strategy for hunting the *bisonete*?" asked a curious Don Bernardo.

"We watched the natives from afar. To down a beast with a bow and arrow is very difficult; they learned to separate a not full-grown beast, but maybe a younger male and scare it to a forward location where they had dug five foot holes, covered with long weeds. Then they'd chase the beast into the foot hole and maim a leg. Then they'd slaughter the beast. "Another technique we spied from afar: a young hunter would disguise himself with a buffalo skin and somehow coax a few buffalo to follow him into running toward a cliff. He'd then jump over a location and hide in a cranny. The buffaloes would fall over the cliff, and typically maim a leg. Or they'd be stunned by the fall and unable to defend themselves. At this point, the awaiting band would ambush these injured beasts and kill them with long pole-knives. Then, the meat was separated from the fur skins and placed on travois to be pulled by the dogs to the primary band." *Cibolero* explained.

"How did you hunt these *bisonetes*?" Don Bernardo asked.

"We did do this: with our horses we would peel off a younger buffalo and mimic the *Querecho* Band. We'd try to maim the beast by shooting a forward leg with our musket guns. Our muskets could not kill a beast. We would then ambush with the large metal *machetes*, and *varas*—lances, aiming at the lower front legs to down the beast. Then we'd strike the neck and under the chest to kill it. The beast was skinned, and large portions of the meat were saddled to be taken back to the base camp, where it would be cut in small slender pieces. It would be smothered in salt and flour, then hung to dry. A great meal would be prepared that day of buffalo steaks and *papitas*—potatoes," *Cibolero* explained.

"While hunting, you were surprised upon by *Apaches-Jicarrilla* at *Wahatoya*?" Don Bernardo asked.

"Yes, they are very protective and aggressive about the plains; their existence is dependent upon the *bisonete*. There were three of us. We were in the low lands, not quite entering the *llano*-prairie, and awaiting the sound of hoofs. We did not follow a herd like the Querechos, so we had to wait and hope they would come by our launching point. Out of nowhere, flying arrows appeared—hitting my friend in the chest. The horses jumped and there was hollering of all sorts," *Cibolero* shared, with fear in his voice.

"How did you escape?" Don Bernardo asked.

"I was standing by my horse. Then I felt this arrow hit my upper chest, my horse jumped, and I naturally grabbed the reins and tried to mount. Then I allowed my horse south to travel south. I broke the arrow shaft and kept riding. My friends did not make it out," *Cibolero* said in despair.

"How did you end up by the *Wahatoya* Mountain?" Don Bernardo asked.

"We followed a river; soon I was losing consciousness. I remember falling next to the river. The next thing I remember is seeing Watili's face," *Cibolero* explained.

"It was fortunate you ran into Watili. I did not realize she had the healing knowledge of the Medicine Man," Don Bernardo observed.

"I wanted to thank you for pulling me out of that mess. Where are you from?" *Cibolero* said. "I recognize your name, Don Bernardo Pacheco y Miera. Were you the cartographer on the *Escalante-Domingues* Expedition?"

Don Bernardo responded, "Yes, the mapmaker. I am originally from Burgoss, Spain." He thought to himself: *funny, never heard of him.*

"We are going to be heading north to Watili's village: this is unchartered territory. Would you come with us?" Don Bernardo asked *Cibolero*.

"I lost my armaments in the skirmish with the Apaches. You have no arms?" *Cibolero* asked.

"That's how it was during the first expedition. We traveled with the *Padres*—Priests. They did not permit any arms whatsoever," Don Bernardo explained.

"You have no *pistola*-pistol, no rifle, no *mosquete*—mosquete?" *Cibolero* asked excitedly. "How will you defend yourself?"

"During the first expedition, we were never felt threatened, never scared. Most natives I've encountered have never seen a fire stick, as they like to call our pistols and rifles. So, they are not threatened when they see us and our horses," Don Bernardo explained.

"These mountain Indians are not as aggressive and territorial as the Apaches we encountered. We lost our bearings, and ended up on the east side of the mountains, facing the prairie lands that belong to the Apaches. I don't want to travel without direction again; once is enough," *Cibolero* said. "I will travel with you and Watili."

Watili had no idea what lands they were talking about or the lengthy boat ride to the new world. Her focus was to return to her family.

The next morning at daybreak, the group awoke and saddled. They would travel south to make it to the heart of this valley, traveling about forty miles per day (or 136 leagues), arriving in present-day Manassa, Colorado.

The slow passage provided time for the three to talk with one another.

Cibolero prodded his horse to go next to Watili, "I want to thank you again. I heard your prayers ongoing all night. Can you tell me what you prayed for?"

She thought to herself: *no one ever asks of my people's prayers, yet they did assist in saving his life.*

Watili slowly answered, "I prayed the prayers and knowledge of my grandfather, the Medicine Man."

"Can you tell me or explain this to me? I believe it helped heal me," *Cibolero* said.

Watili looked at him and shared this old *Ute* prayer:

"Earth teach me stillness as the grasses are stilled with light
Earth teach me the suffering as old stones with memory
Earth teach me humility as blossoms are humble with grinning
Earth teach me as the caring mother secures her young
Earth teach me as the tree stand alone and as the limitation of the ant that crawls on the ground
Earth teach me the freedom as the eagle which soars in the sky."

"Are you connected to Nature with your prayers?" *Cibolero* asked.

"Whatever befalls Earth, befalls the son and daughters of Earth," she answered.

"I do not understand. You used plants and extracts to heal my wounds, and then used prayers to earth to enhance this healing? How does that work?" *Cibolero* asked.

"Earth is our mother. Whatever befalls Earth, befalls the sons and daughter of Earth. If men spit upon the ground, they spit upon themselves." Watili answered pointedly.

"So, there is a Oneness: a connection between men, women and Earth?" *Cibolero* said, trying to understand this Oneness.

"This we know. All things are connected, like the blood that unites one family. All things are connected. We did not weave the web of life. We are merely a strand in it. Whatever we do to the web, we do to ourselves," Watili explained.

"Your prayers to Earth and use of plants to heal me are of the same strand?" *Cibolero* asked.

"Yes," answered Watili.

Cibolero nodded his head in approval. He may have grasped this understanding of Nature, man, and the interconnected Oneness. He knew this understanding of the Web of Life had saved him.

The prairie-toughened cowboy *Cibolero* then prodded his horse forward, smiling as he trotted circles around Watili and her horse. A transformative moment had overtaken *Cibolero*: the ah-ha moment had overtaken this tough-as-nails vaquero. He felt he had been healed by Mother Earth's herbs, and a Native prayer that worked through Watili to save his life.

"Watili, I must tell you," a giggly and astonished *Cibolero* said, "I realize and see now that it is Mother Earth who truly provides life." A moment of discovery had overtaken the *vaquero*.

"What does that mean to you?" the knowledgeable Watili asked.

"Mother Earth is the healer." *Cibolero* said. "I would never have thought your healing remedies would work on me, Watili," *Cibolero* said.

Don Bernardo witnessed this transformation; he was taken aback by this sinewy cowboy's reaction to Watili's healing skills.

Don Bernardo heard the conversation and was enthralled, but said nothing.

Then Don Bernardo said, "On the expedition five years ago, we came across many different Indians."

"Were they of the same band? *Cibolero* asked.

"Not really. Each had different customs, yet most spoke Yuta: the primary *Ute* language. All could sign with other bands. Yet some also spoke Comanche or some Apache, depending if they were a trading partner to a distance band. They were called *Anamuchis-Cosinas, Putatmmumis, Payuches, Moqui, Oraybi, Xongopabi, Gualpi, Parussi, Yamparicas*, and *Lagunas*. We made it all the way north to the Salt Lake. The closer a band is to a lake, the more they depend on fish as their primary food. They become less dependent on herbs, vegetables, and red meat," Don Bernardo said. "Almost all wore long sleep shirts and pants made of either hares or rabbits."

"They are all very effective traders of their goods, whether it be herbs, black berries, manania, venison, cockcherry, piñon nuts, maize, dates, pottery, or rabbit skins. As you go further north you find dried tuna cakes, fresh tuna, dried seed for atole, porcupines, watermelons, cantaloupes, and squash." Don Bernardo explained.

"What did you trade with them?" *Cibolero* asked.

"Carne Seca—dried meat, and especially buffalo meat, was in demand. What they really liked were clear and colored beads; this was a premium item to them, they had never seen such things. I guess it could be a good gift to impress a wife or girlfriend!" Don Bernardo

chuckled. "That dynamic never changes, wherever you are in the New World."

"How did you speak with them?" *Cibolero* asked.

"We had translators with us. We would trade *carne seca*-dried salted beef for information and directions to the next band. Sometimes they would escort us there. If they could not understand a band's language, they could sign with them. We always asked who the next band would be, and how far we'd have to travel to meet them," Don Bernardo explained.

"What type of structures can we expect to see?" *Cibolero* asked.

"No, you are thinking of the established adobe structures in the Santa Fe vicinity. What you will see here are very small, undeveloped villages. The structures you will see is how Watili saved your life within the *choza*—the reed hut. These are mobile village; they will move to a new location, dependent on safety and the season. What you will witness is very fragile and dependent upon Nature to survive. They only harvest what they need, and do not exploit a crop, so the next person can use it. It is a very fragile environment: really quite beautiful."

As the sun began to descend, a green light was seen facing due west, dancing in all directions, yet staying stationary.

"Let us draw camp here," said Don Bernardo. As the group made camp and campfire, the green dancing lights were still in the distance as the night grew dark. Then the dancing green lights suddenly appeared above the group, appearing to study them.

Don Bernardo yelled, "*Jesús nos salva*—Jesus please save us!"

Cibolero shielded his eyes and screamed, "*Abrahim, nos guarda*—Abraham, safeguard us!"

Watili fell to her knees and bowed, "*Senawaha*, help us." *Senawaha* was the god of the *Utes*.

Then, the lights suddenly disappeared.

The group just looked at each other and said nothing. All calmly went to sleep.

For the next few days, the group traversed mountains and valleys until they arrived at present-day Dolores, Colorado, and located the original route of the Dominquez-Escalante Expedition.

Dolores River Discussion

At the Dolores River (near Dolores, Colorado), the group camped and found the original route of the Dominguez-Escalante Trail. In the early morning, they began to follow the river north.

"I named this river *Rio de Nuestro Señora de Dolores*—River of our Lady of Sorrow, after we discovered its route," said Don Bernardo.

"How can you name a river that has already been named? We called this river the *Weeminuche*, after the band that dominated this area," said Watili. "The *Weeminuche* have been here forever. (1500 B.C.). They are descendants of the *Anasazi* people. They named all these rivers, creeks, and mountains ranges. Everything had names."

"Well, the name was not posted!" Don Bernardo snapped.

"You never even had the courtesy to ask if the river had a name, did you?" Watili shot back.

"You named all the rivers, valleys, and mountains ranges when you were on the expedition?" asked *Cibolero*. "Were there not bandsmen that you could ask?"

"We have claimed this land in the name of Christ and the Spanish Crown, as you well know," countered Don Bernardo. "We are discovering this new land, and the natives are under our sovereignty now. The Crown provided me with the authority to name all of this new land."

"What have you discovered?" Watini asked again. "The *Ute* people have been in this area for over two thousand years. We are a sovereign people with our own laws and customs. We respect Nature and live with the land." The group rode the entire day and finally camped for the evening.

The night grew dark; the flames in the fire began to dwindle. All fell asleep.

As morning approached, bright sunlight broke over the crest of the large, flat rock the group had slept beneath for safety. The sunlight awoke both *Cibolero* and Don, only for them to hear the hiss of breathing from atop the rock.

Watali was performing sun-salutation exercises atop the rock in the early morning. She started facing north, her palms centered on her heart in a prayer pose. She lifted her hands straight up and then wide, requesting in prayer that *Senawah* protect her journey and allow her to see her family. She bent at the waist, trailing her hands behind her, as she exhaled. Her prayers steadily rose like a droning buzz over the morning landscape. She then placed her hands squarely on the face of the rock, and her legs shifted back until her torso was flat as a board. Her knees then bent forward, and she twisted herself around until she faced upward and to the east, with her hands clasped and raised in a salutation to the sun. Her words were clear and distinct:

From the East:
I Seek the Lessons of Childhood: to see with the Trusting Innocence of a Small One,
The Lessons of Spirit, Given in Love by our Creator.
From the South:
To Learn the Ways of Questioning:
The Fire and Dependence of Adolescence
the Truths, and how They Help us Grow Along This Path.
From the West:
Where the Grandfathers Teach us Acceptance of Responsibility
that Comes During the Years of Marriage and Family

That my own Children Grow Strong and True.
From the North:
Where the Elders, who by Their Long Lives
Have Learned and Stored Wisdom and Knowledge.
and Learned to Walk in Balance and Harmony with our Mother, Earth.

"Not quite the uneducated savages you thought them to be, eh, Don Bernardo?" said *Cibolero*, elbowing his companion in the ribs. "Reminds me of the ancient *Raja Yoga*: the exercise of enlightenment from India."

Don Bernardo viewed this entire routine and just shook his head.

Not long after, Watili returned from her exercise and prayers, and the trio began preparing for the next leg of the journey.

After a few miles, hugging the rim of the mountain ridge upon their horses in the early morning, Watili pulled on the reins of her horse.

"E*scucha*—listen!" she said.

Ears straining, in the background over a ridge they heard a sound, unlike any other sound heard in these lands.

Don Bernardo said, "*Cibolero*, hold our horses!" as Watili and himself dismantled and began to creep quickly over the ridge toward the sound. They followed a ravine toward the sound, and climbed a short hill that overlooked the area.

Don Bernardo was shocked by what he saw. Below them there was a mining operation complete with cutting stones, pull-carts with wheels, and the grinding sound of cutting rock—all manpowered with small horses and managed by natives.

"Since when do Indians use wheels?" he asked Watili. "What band is this? And what are they doing with equipment of this kind?"

"These are the Southern *Utes*, the *Weeminuche* again," answered Watili in a low voice. "We must go. They will not like either one of us here." Both quietly scurried back to their horses.

Cilolero was awaiting anxiously, "What was that sound?"

Don Bernardo, "A mining operation. We must leave now!"

They mounted their horses and briskly continued on their journey.

"Since when do the Indians have mining operations?" *Cibolero* asked, as he spurred his horse to catch up to the shocked riders.

"Since when do Indians use wheels?" a still surprised Don Bernardo repeated his question. "That group has been working with Spanish miners. They are using their tools and techniques."

The group finally felt safe enough to slow down once they were a few miles from the mining operation. They slowed their gallop and took in the beauty of the mountain range, enjoying the clean air they were breathing. *Cibolero* drew his horse next to Waltili.

"Tell me about your people?" the *Cibolero* asked a surprised Watili.

She glanced at him and then looked forward, not knowing if she could trust him to answer this question honestly, coming as it did from a white man she barely knew. Yet, somehow, she knew she could open her heart and share her personal journey with him. His eyes focused on her, yet he waited patiently for a response.

"Living in *Parussi*, everyone is busy. We exist with Nature. I would help my mother in all things: if we were not collecting berries or piñon, we were skinning rabbits, or sewing shirts and pants for my brother and father. We lived in the small *chozas*, but we spent most of our time outside with Nature. "

"How did you learn to heal?" the *Cibolero* was still clearly stunned by the native skills that had saved his life.

"I spent much of my time with my mother's father: my medicine man grandfather. He would take me outside of the village to gather roots, herbs, and other plants that grew only in remote places or near certain rivers. Certain plants only bloom during exact times of the season, and you have to there at that time to collect their powers," she explained.

"He shared this knowledge with you?"

"Yes. Sometimes we would run into a medicine man from another village. That was always interesting. They would trade herbs and plants, then smoke from their pipes and get all happy!" Watili giggled at the memory of these original herb traders. This train of thought carried her on until suddenly, she was talking aloud about her grandfather.

"It was his habit to always collect healing plants with a prayer, requesting permission to use the plants for medicinal-healing purposes. Sometimes he would kneel and touch the root or flower to his forehead before pulling them from the soil."

"He prayed to the plant?" a questioning *Cibolero* looked skeptical.

"My grandfather prayed to the Creator for a blessing in using the plants for healing," she explained.

"This is a very different life than living in a hacienda," the *Cibolero* mused.

"Listen, living in El Paso with a family as a slave girl, it has been fair to me." she responded.

"What do you mean 'fair'?" he asked.

"*Yo soy un esclavo*—I am a slave. I may never have freedom, yet the family I live with treated me respectfully."

"I asked you what your people are like?" *Cibolero* asked again.

"This you must understand. I do not feel the freedom of Parussi; you must understand this to comprehend my people." Watili explained. "In the hacienda in El Paso, all of the slave girls were busy. We worked hard all day gardening, canning, washing clothes, butchering animals, and preparing meals, all with the hope of one day being emancipated. Watili paused for a moment.

"Then on Sunday, we go to Mass, and I have learned to have Jesus in my heart. With the Spanish, we learned to pray for faith. But in *Parussi*, we live the faith," Watili explained.

"Explain that: *Parussi* live the faith," *Cibolero* was puzzled by her answer.

"In *Parussi*, we rely on Earth to provide the water of the *rito*—creek, the natural crops of berries, piñon, sap from the trees, corn, and long weeds from the fields to live upon. This is all created by the Creator, who is faith–there is a Oneness with one another." Watili explained.

"But you have learned and felt that faith comes through Jesus," *Cibolero* observed.

"Yes, but it is different than a direct relationship with Nature: a direct relationship with the Creator itself. You call him God the Father. Yet in *Parussi*, the closeness of the relationship between Nature and myself—the Creator and myself, is something that is felt internally: a Oneness with Nature."

Cibolero grasped this concept, "It is this mutual dependency on Nature that conceived the Oneness with the Creator who forever links you to Mother Earth." Internally, *Cibolero* then thought to himself: *maybe that is why the natives live in similar manners to the way they lived hundreds of years in the past.*

A surprised Watili looked at him, "I am surprised you understand this concept."

"In El Paso, in a village life, there is not a dependency on Mother Earth; therefore exists a gap to conjoining to the Oneness." *Cibolero* further perceived.

An enlightened Don Bernardo, the slaver, just listened to the conversation.

Encounter with
(*Yutas Barbones*) Beaded Utes

For the next leg of the journey, they closely followed the path of the rugged mountains along the southwest corner of Colorado. They rode one day, and did not come across any bandsmen through the day or night. The next day, following the *Escalante-Dominquez* Map, they traversed east into canyon land. Don Bernardo said, "This is the way we went, but those canyons up ahead do not look familiar." He made the decision to pursue the trail into the diagonal pathways of the canyon for a couple of miles before he realized they were lost.

Cibolero doubtfully eyed the high walls surrounding them. "This does not look like it has an ending. Do we keep going?"

Don Bernardo began to get nervous. He instinctively knew, like an eagle that attacks its prey from above, a Native scouting party would take advantage of a high position and attack the trio with arrows in hopes of obtaining the horses they rode. To be lost in such a captive canyon for any length of time was foolhardy and dangerous. Don Bernardo knew he was being watched. He dismounted from his horse, and immediately told *Cibolero* to gather some dry firewood.

As Don Bernardo grabbed *ocate* from his saddle bags and began collecting small twigs to light a fire, *Cibolero* arrived with dry scrub, small, broken branches, and thick tree trunk pieces. He did not understand why or how these were necessary, but the cowboy did as he was told.

As Don Bernardo blew on the small fire to create smoke, the flames rose and the fire danced in all directions. Gently, he began feeding the pieces of wood to the fire. Don Bernardo thought to himself: *this is how bands inform neighboring bands a visitor is forthcoming: a smoke signal. But today this is a map to get out of the canyon.*

As the smoke rose, it lifted straight up the narrow canyon walls and gathered near the high tops of the upper rocks. Watili, *Cibolero* and Don Bernardos simply watched the gray smoke rise. As the smoke swirled within the canyon walls, it caught a breeze and went straight backwards, following a path of freedom from where it had come.

Elated, Don Bernardo said, "Get on your horses; we have to follow that smoke and get out, or we could be left high and dry in this dangerous canyon."

They all jumped on their horses and began following the smoke as it trailed along just above the canyon. Finally, after a few minutes, the opening to the canyon appeared. "Like I told you, the passage out of trouble," said Don Bernardo proudly, gesturing toward their escape. Watili and *Cibolero* just smiled at each other. "How did you know this?" asked Watili.

"Just a little Indian trick I picked up, usually done as a warning, but it works well to get out of trouble and into the mouth of the canyon," Don Bernardo replied with a grin.

The three picked up the pace a bit and traveled until midday, finally stopping near Olathe, Colorado. They could see a party traveling in the distance.

Don Bernardo said in excitement, "*Yutas Barbones!*—Bearded Utes!"

Cibolero could not believe what his eyes were seeing.

"That is not possible," said Cibolero. Watili just smiled at their amazement.

Approaching them quickly were Natives with long beards and hairy arms and legs. This was very uncommon among native people. The fully-bearded men looked like *Capuchin Padres* or *Bethlehemites*—raggedly dressed first century inhabitants of *Bethlehem*.

Watili knew them as the Bearded *Utes* or *"Tirangapui"* in her native tongue. Seeing these hairy men, she knew she was getting closer to her home. Watili knew her role; she warmly greeted the *Tirangapui*, or *Barbones*, in her native *Ute* language.

The *Barbones*, upon spotting the trio, were startled as well. They were aware of the stories about the big dog (the mighty horse), but had never seen one in person.

"What is that animal?" asked the leader of the *Barbones*.

"It is a horse. It comes from another land far away from here; we ride this horse to move from one location to another," explained Watili, as she dismounted to show them the four-legged animal. "Where are you headed?" she asked after a moment's hesitation.

"We are going to the big river to trade for items for our village," answered the man. As a shrewd trader, he asked, "Do you have any items to trade? Can we trade for your animal?"

Watili laughed a bit, and asked Don Bernardo and *Cibolero* if they wanted to trade with these men.

Cibolero brought out a small metal knife with a wooden handle, its blade shining in the afternoon sun.

The *Barbones'* keen eyes opened wide at this new item. They looked at each other as if to say: *we want that knife.*

The *Barbones* backed off a few steps. They turned their backs to these horse people; they reached into their hemp bags, with their flowing beards swaying in the summer breeze, and quietly talked to each other—planning to make an offer for the knife. They then returned with two small bags in their hands.

The *Barbone* rubbed his beard, and then offered one of the bags to Watili. She took it and opened it, her eyes opening wide with surprise: this was an item she had only heard of.

"What is it?" Don Bernardo asked.

"*Hedlondilla* leaves and root—*Chaparral*. It is a very rare medicinal plant," Watili explained. "This has great value in this land as a tea, or you can slowly chew on the root."

Cibolero asked, "What does it heal?"

"Depending on how it is prepared, either snake-bite fever or other high fevers; even joint pains, if slowly digested as a whole. If taken as a tea, it cures stomach aches, bowel cramps, colds, and flu," she explained.

His arrow-wound experience had taught *Cibolero* the value of herbal Native remedies.

"I'll take that," he said.

Watili told the *Barbones*, "The trade is acceptable. What is in the second bag?"

Barone smiled. "Piñon seeds," he said as he held up this special treat. He gave both bags to Watili. *Cibolero* handed the knife to the happy traders and they smiled, admiring their trade.

Out of a mountain crevasse that shadowed the trail, a strange-looking man appeared, dressed in rabbit fur over his loins and shoulders, a deer hat with small protruding horns, deer bladders hung on a belt across his chest, and a walking stick with a dried snake skin curled around the shaft. Don Bernardo, Cibolero, and Watili were taken aback by this strange man—who seemed to have appeared out of nowhere.

The *Barbones* said to him, "What are you doing here, Medicine Man?" The stranger was indeed a medicine man, on the hunt for rare medicinal remedies in the canyon. "I have been following this group for some time now. I first spotted them in the rock canyon with their big dogs," the medicine man said, as he approached the standing group, marveling at the power and muscle of the horses.

Watili spoke up. "What type of plants were you pursuing?"

The medicine man knew, by that type of questioning, that the girl had realized he was searching for something specific: a plant she thought grew in a barren canyon. But it was not a plant he was searching for. He smiled as he answered, "I search for an eagle's nest: the broken shells of a chick's new birth, high in the canyon walls."

Watili was astonished. "You go to great risk climbing the canyon walls to locate the eagle's nest. That mother eagle will tear you to pieces and pluck your eyes out if she sees you near her nest!" She studied him intently for a moment before understanding dawned in her eyes. "You will use the broken shells of the hatched eggs as part of a ceremony in celebration of young girls becoming women. You are a *Shaman*."

The medicine man looked keenly at Watili. "You have the knowledge of healing."

Watili would not be sidetracked from her line of questioning. "You have found eagle feathers, haven't you?" she stared intently at him.

The medicine man just smiled at her. Eagle feathers are a very powerful symbol, believed to provide soaring insight.

"Last night, I dreamt a vision where I saw these large dogs—these horses, you call them—pulling a wood *choza* with round shields," (a wagon with wheels, Watili realized), "Making much ruckus and changing with ways of the world we live in." The medicine man's eyes glazed as he shared his vision.

Watili's face darkened, knowing all too well such truth existed in *El Paso*. She had not thought it would happen in this area, so close to her home in *Parussi*.

The *Barbones* just looked at the medicine man, consternation wrinkling their brows as they wondered whether the medicine man's vision could come true. Finally, after some more small bartering, they walked away with the medicine man accompanying them.

Don Bernardo's party continued out of the canyon and camped a few miles north, with the hopes of making it to the big river the next day.

Colorado River-Passage to the Pacific

El Rio de Nuestros Señora de Dolores—The Las Animas River in southeastern Colorado, was the river the group intended to follow on the next leg of their journey. Don Bernardo had crossed this river many times, near Dolores, Colorado, and had spent time there five years earlier, with the purpose of finding the western river passage to the Pacific Ocean.

The group awoke just before daybreak with the hopes of getting to the big river before sundown. Don Bernardo thought they could make it in one day if they embarked on the slender pathway that led due north. The group stopped only briefly on this leg of the trail, and by mid-afternoon the sound of the big river could be heard in the distance. Toward the end of the day, they arrived at the *Rio de San Colorado* (Saint Colorado River in present-day Grand Junction, Colorado). Don Bernardo smiled and prodded his horse into the thirty-foot-wide deep waters of the river. The horse swam across to the other side with its entire body submerged under the water, its nose snorting for air as Don Bernardo hung onto the horn. Watili and *Cibolero* followed. When they all reached the other side at last, they dismounted and examined their wet clothes.

"That is the widest and deepest river we crossed on this journey," said Don Bernardo as the group shed jackets and outer-garments, hoping to dry off. They tied the reins of their horses to small tree limbs. "Walk with me," Don Bernardo said. He and *Cibolero* walked along the river banks, hoping the afternoon sun would dry them off. Watili followed a few paces behind the two men.

"This is the Western Passage to the Pacific Ocean or the Gulf of *Mexico*," Don Bernardo began.

"How do you know?" *Cibolero* asked.

"I measured the depth and width of the water, here and downstream. It is 41°-4 latitude. This is the only waterway with the depth and width to carry the distance to the West Coast."

Excited, *Cibolero* cried, "You found the Western Passage! The Crown must have been very excited to hear about this."

"I did not report it." Don Bernardo's tone was matter-of-fact.

"What? Was that not your purpose? To locate this passage?" *Cibolero* was overly excited by this news. "Don't you see vast opportunity here?"

"I knew that once this immaculate place is recognized as the passage to the western Pacific, the innocent relationship between these natives and Nature will never return," said Don Bernardo.

"You didn't seem to care about this relationship five years ago, on the original expedition," *Cibolero* said.

"Yes, you are right. Initially, I did feel that way, but after the expedition, I realized what I was really seeing. That is why I wrote nothing in my reports to the Crown. This is one of the reasons I am returning Watili to her band," Don Bernardo explained. He turned and looked back at the river. "Listen," he said after a silent moment, "We must travel northwest before dark. There is a friendly band of *Cosinanas* we can stay with." As they walked back and mounted their horses to continue the journey, *Cibolero* just looked at Don Bernardo, not fully understanding his motives.

They rode anther hour before night fell, and then they made camp. A somber Don Bernardo could not believe they had trekked back to the river along the Western Passage to the Pacific.

Daybreak arrived. Don Bernardo said, "Let's sleep in, we are visiting a friendly band; let us not arrive too early."

Close to mid-morning, the group mounted their horses and rode until they arrived at Fruita, Colorado, at a *rancheria* (village) that surprised both Watili and Cibolero.

On the outskirts of the village were well-organized, irrigated fields that grew maize, pinto beans, squash, watermelons, cantaloupe, and peach trees. The fields were irrigated from small *acequias* (creeks). There were meadows of orchard trees such as apple, *capolin* (choke cherries), and pears; in the distance, a growth of piñon graced the landscape. These farming techniques were sufficient to feed a small village, without bandsman ever leaving to hunt game or pick wild plants. *Cibolero* and Watili were amazed by these farming techniques.

As the trio neared the village, vertical fences built of five-foot-high stick corrals held domestic herds of mountain-goats and turkeys. Structures of stone, mud, or adobe demonstrated that this band lived here year-round.

As the group began to enter the village, they dismounted and waited, so as not alarm the band with their horses. Very soon after, a young boy spotted them from a distance. The young boy ran to notify the *Cosinanas's Cacique* (Chief).

The *Cacique* walked out of his adobe home, and stopped in his tracks as he saw the large animals with the long legs: a big dog, or so he thought. Then, he walked to the group with the others of his band following him. He recognized Don Bernardo and smiled, and he signed him to approach.

Watili stepped forward, and in her *Ute* language said, "Good morning, *Cacique*."

The *Cacique* answered, "Good morning," as he and the group pondered and mused at the long-legged animals and saddle bags. Still, as chief, he asked them to follow him into his home. He looked hard at *Cibolero*, squinting his eyes to look closely at the curly red hair under the cowboy hat. He had never seen red hair before.

The group followed the *Cacique* into the village. *Cibolero* found a small stream of water, and took care of the horses while the others entered the adobe home. The hardened dirt floors gave way to a large room with a belly fireplace, serving to keep the room warm with piñon firewood. The group sat on the floor.

The *Cacique* lifted the lid of a small wooden box, and took out a cigarette to enjoy with both Watili and Don Bernardo. This cigarette was made of a smoked cactus leaf and wild-berry juice.

His first question was, "Tobacco?" Don Bernardo smiled and nodded an assent, for he knew this was a premium commodity to the bands, especially if the tobacco had originated from the American south states of Kentucky or North Carolina.

He then asked, "*Tatas?*" in reference to the priests who had accompanied Don Bernardo on the first trip.

Don Bernardo shook his head and said, "No."

The Cacique explained to Watili as she translated, "The *tatas* were very nice to his people, but he did not want his villagers to be Christians."

Cacique then asked Don Bernardo, "Your friend outside ... why does he not look like you?"

Don Bernardo answered, "He is from my home country of Spain."

Cacique noted, "He is from a different people than you are from. He does not carry the same spirit."

Don Bernardo did not understand what he meant.

The woman in the adobe then brought warm food to eat in a wooden bowl with eating utensils, things Don Bernardo did not think existed with *Indios*. Inside the bowl was warm *atole* with prunes. The woman took a plate and spoon to Cibolero, and returned with smile on her face, saying something about his red locks.

The Cacique then got down to business: "What do you have to trade? As you can see, we have a developed village and many braves to defend our home. Do you have fire sticks?"

Don Bernardo answered, "As with my first expedition, we do not carry fire sticks. However, I brought tobacco for you and something you have not seen: crystal beads." He turned to Watili and murmured in her ear, "Please bring these items from Cibolero's saddle bags."

Watili returned and gave both pouches to Don Bernardo. Her dark eyes darted between Don and the Cacique the entire time, watching and learning how a trade exchange takes place between two men.

Don Bernardo opened one of the pouches, and the wonderful aroma of tobacco from the deep south of Kentucky filled the room. The *Cacique* smiled, for he knew this was a special treat. Don Bernardo handed him the pouch, and the *Cacique* put his entire nose (and it was ridiculously large, or so Watili thought) into the pouch, inhaled, and knew that this gift was from another land. He then reached into his wooden box and pulled out a skinned, dry, cactus leaf and placed a *punio* (small handful) of tobacco into the leaf, rolled it, and then moistened the edges with his tongue to seal the cigarette. He then grabbed a small wooden stick from the fire, and lit his creation with a friendly gesture.

He sat back and inhaled this relaxing *toke* (smoke) and said, "I will trade you my premium turkey bunch for one of your long-legged animals." He said this knowing the animal was rarely seen in these areas.

Don Bernardo smiled and courteously shook his head, saying, "No, we would only like to stay here tonight. We are traveling to Watili's village." He then opened the second bag and extracted a *punio* of clear and green crystal beads, and placed these in the hand of the *Cacique*.

The *Cacique* was surprised as he looked closely at the little spheres. He turned swiftly and immediately gave one to the woman in his adobe. She grinned, speaking to him in a low but cheerful tone, then walked off and out of the adobe, maybe to show her sisters her new treasure. Jewelry, for some reason, has this effect on women of all bands.

"You can stay here tonight!" *Cacqiue* immediately responded. Don Bernardo thanked him warmly.

Don Bernardo, Watili, and *Cacique* walked out of the adobe. There were three young and pretty *cosinanas* (maidens) smiling and admiring the red locks of *Cibolero*. Watili was jealous and she ordered snappishly, "Get those horses behind this adobe and feed them." *Cibolero* took this order in stride and followed this unpleasant request. The pretty *cosinanas* shot Watili a blank stare, a form of sign language only women understand. Then they walked off, muttering something to one another.

Don Bernardo, Watili, and *Cibolero* spent the day walking the village. Everyone had chores, and all chores got done or the system would not function for the community. One small group would be skinning a deer, mountain goat, or rabbit. The hide would then be given to the tanners, who would stretch the hides and tan the underside of the skin. The skin was handed off to the seamstresses of the band, who would sew together pants or long-sleeved shirts of all sizes. The meat was shared throughout the camp. Everyone benefitted.

Even more impressive were the six-foot-high vertical stick structures with horizontal reed interior walls that let the sun's warmness enter, but kept the cold mountain air outside. These walls were used as a drying place for meats, fruits, vegetables, and medicinal plants. The amount of dry goods in this large space could feed a small village for an entire winter. Watili looked closely at the medicinal plants, hanging alone, and separated from all other commodities. She thought to herself: *these plants and roots can cure any illness*. The thought brought to mind her grandfather.

The irrigated rows of fields all faced south to take advantage of the many sunny days of the short summer cycle. The organization and well-kept, clean rows with healthy, deep, rich soil was managed by rotating different crops in each field each season.

The visiting group marveled at the efficiency of the village's operation. In the evening, they retired to an empty adobe structure near the *Cacique's* own adobe to rest and ready themselves for the next day. In the early morning, the group awoke and readied for the journey.

As the group was mounting and preparing to leave, the *Cacique* stopped the group with one request. It was clear the poor man was terribly embarrassed.

He looked directly at *Cibolero*. "My woman … she would like a lock of your hair," he said shyly.

Cibolero grinned and, sweeping his hat from his head, bent over the neck of his horse. The Cacique's woman ran up to the *vaquero*, clipped a lock, and walked back into the adobe home. The group rode off.

The Gualpi Village

The group rode another eighteen hours as they followed Don Bernardo into a secluded canyon where he expected to locate the *Gualpi* village near Meeker, Colorado. Don Bernardo said to *Cibolero*, "This *Gualpi* band is at war with the *Apache Navajos* from northeastern Arizona and New *Mexico*. The *Apache Navajos* have decimated their village by capturing and enslaving many of their people. They want to form an alliance for war with the Spanish to punish and avenge this act."

"Would the Spanish form such an alliance?" asked *Cibolero*.

"Yes, the Spanish would do this if they could control the territory. The *Gualpi* would need to submit to the Catholic faith and be under the control of the Spanish Crown." Don Bernardo explained. "The Crown is considering treaties in this same fashion to form alliances with other bands in other territories."

As the canyon narrowed, warriors could be seen ahead, standing with bows at the ready, awaiting this group's arrival. This startled Watili and *Cibolero*.

"How did they know we were arriving?" *Cibolero* asked nervously.

"Smoke signals," answered Don Bernardo, as he scooted ahead and stopped the group before the warriors. He gave the bandsmen the sign of peace, and then the trio dismounted their horses.

From the side of the canyon wall, the *Gualpi Cacique* stepped out onto the pathway. He recognized Don Bernardo, but not the two others. His manner was far from friendly, even bordering on hostile. Watili stepped forward and translated the *Yutas* language to Don Bernardo.

"Since you were here years back, this land has suffered many attacks by *Apaches* from the Southern Territory," the *Cacique* said. Gone were the naïve days of the natives, in which the Spanish priests and their companions could walk into a village and share their stories of Jesus of Nazareth, love and compassion. The natives learned that not long after these visits, a rage-filled warrior class on horseback would arrive to enslave a village.

"Do you have the authority to speak directly to the Spanish Crown?" the knowing *Cacique* asked.

"I do not." Don Bernardo answered the chief softly, as to not upset him.

"Can you take me to Santa Fe to negotiate an alliance?" the *Cacique* asked.

Don Bernardo shook his head. "No."

"Then get yourself out of this land, for more like you mean an end to our existence," the *Cacique* said.

The group mounted their horses and departed, feeling lucky to leave unharmed. As they left the mouth of canyon and looked back to assure they would not be followed, they felt relieved and safe.

Cibolero rode in silence, pondering something he had thought. Suddenly, he drew up his horse and looked sternly at Don Bernardo. "I remember you provided a report to the Spanish Crown and maybe high-level officials in *El Paso*, but did your map disclose the location of these Indian villages to anyone else?"

Don Bernardo did not answer.

Watili pulled up her horse, suddenly understanding the entire situation: the map-maker had delivered the route to *Ute* villages to the slavers. Rage exploded inside of her like a wildfire, and she screamed incomprehensible words in *Utas*. The horses were spooked and became jittery and unmanageable, turning in all directions.

Cibolero started circling Don Bernardo on his horse, threateningly. The *vaquero's* head ached with the immensity of what had just been revealed.

"You're here for the gold and silver! You could care less about these people, these '*innocent people and this land*' as you like to say. You knew the knowledge of routes and location of profitable mines could guarantee you safe passage from the Crown to travel through and find this ore," *Cibolero* said. He reined in his horse beside Don Bernardo, considering the situation.

"These maps you draw, the journals you write … the medicine man at Box Canyon was right! Wagons would wipe out our *rancherias*—our villages. He was right about you! You have betrayed all my Indian people!" Watili shrieked at Don Bernardo.

Slowly, it dawned on *Cibolero* that the land would someday be exploited by Don Bernardo-like-types; even the vast herds of buffalo he loved to hunt would disappear. His voice cracked with rage. "The *bisonete*-buffalo ... you will slaughter many. They will have no ranges in which to run!" Despite his anger, there was a cool, calculating side to *Cibolero*, and even then it was thinking: *if I left with Watili, there would be a good chance we would get lost and not survive. I am not certain Watili knows her way home!* Begrudgingly, he admitted to himself they needed Don Bernardo's knowledge of the trail and reading of the maps to ride out of the mountainous lands alive.

Don Bernardo answered, "I want to take Watili to her village, and yes, I do want to locate special ore. I thought I could do both. Slavery is just part of the Indian life."

Watili was beside herself, sobbing, losing of her breath, as she slowly struggled to control the jittery, nervous horse.

"*Tranquila, tranquila. calmate*—calm down," *Cibolero* spoke soothingly to Watili, as he calmed both her and the horse. Emotions ran high as he turned his horse towards Don Bernardo.

"My community does not allow slavery in any form," *Cibolero* said coldly.

"Your community is the same as mine. Slavery is a way of life for these people. Look at the *Apaches* and *Comanches*, how they raid and have enslaved each other for centuries now!" scoffed Don Bernardo.

"No, we are not. I am from the Jewish tradition, we do not enslave," *Cibolero* said with conviction, at last revealing his true identity. "The imprint on my saddle is an pomegranate, this links to the Jewish mystics and the Kabalah."

"I have seen and felt the *cura*—curing—of Earth from Watili's healing skills. There is a more organic soul in these people than anyone from Europe possesses, yet you will not recognize this. Their souls are entwined with Nature. This you refuse to see!" *Cibolero* pressed.

Don Bernardo just glared at him, "That chief said you were from a different spirit. Now I know what he meant." He prodded his horse forward to continue the journey.

Cibolero and Watili looked at one another; they knew they needed Don Bernardo as a ticket for safe passage and to locate Watili's village. They were still angry, though, and they did not speak to him again. After two silent hours of riding, Don Bernardo pulled up on his horse and made a sign they would make camp for the evening.

He started the fire for warmth, and after supper all three just stared at the flames dancing in the rock circle. Don Bernardo glared at the flames and said, "Now I understand."

Watili snapped, "Understand what?" thinking he was going to talk about slavery.

"Remember the circling green light that appeared above us when we camped at the opening of the mountain (present-day *La Veta* Pass at Fort Garland, Colorado) right before we crossed into the prairie? That light was studying us."

"What for?" a disbelieving *Cibolero* asked.

"That light had never seen a Christian, an Indian and a *Judio*-Jew travel as a group before. I was scared and said 'Christ', you said 'Abraham', and Watili cried out '*Senawah*', all of which are our separate Gods," Don Bernardo explained.

Cibolero raised his voice and pointed his index finger directly at Don Bernardo. "There is only One Higher Being God."

All three pondered the event as they fell asleep. They were now within a two-day ride of Watili's *Parussi* village.

Watili's village - The Parussi

In the morning, the group began the final leg of the journey to Watili's village, named after their own language, *Parussi*. A small *rancheria* (village of reed *chozas*) populated a broad meadow area. The band lived mostly on a plant-based diet, combined with occasional rabbit and deer meat. The primary foods were maize and *calabazas* (squash and wild berries).

The group traveled the entire day. Watili said, "We should camp here," at a site just previous to arriving in her village. She now recognized the mountains and valleys of her homeland.

In the early morning, they crossed the *Rio del Pilar,* then ascended a low *mesa* between crags of shiny, black rock. Arriving at good, open country, they crossed a plain, which toward the east possessed a chain of very high mesas. To the west lay hills covered with *chamiso* (sagebush and red sand). The men followed Watili, went to the edge of the mesas, and finished moving over good, level land. They continued on, entering a canyon along a creek named *Arroyo de Tarey*, with Watili in the lead. Coming out of this canyon, they stopped at the entrance of the next canyon. Watili asked all to dismount.

Cibolero thought to himself: *you could never find this location without a detailed map.*

Watili told Don Bernardo, "I want you to stay in that tree patch and attend to the horses. *Cibolero* and I will enter this canyon and talk to the people of my village. We'll come and get you later." She no longer trusted Don Bernardo's motives.

Don Bernardo looked at Watili and said nothing; he knew his life depended on her word now.

Watili and *Cibolero* began the one-mile walk through the rough, unmarked trail with slender pathways, trees, and bushes in every direction. The trail finally gave way to a pathway to her village. She excitedly began to walk faster, her eyes focused on seeing her village and family. Finally, they arrived at the outside of the village. She began to run. *I cannot believe I am home*, she thought to herself.

She startled a few working villagers, who stopped to see this woman they recognized, but they were confused by her arrival. They stopped what they were doing, and walked to the pathway to see this sight. Then, they yelled at the top of their lungs, "Watili! You have returned."

They gave Watili a hug, with tears and smiles flowing in all directions. *Cibolero* stopped at the entrance, so as not to alarm the braves who were looking at him. The *Parussi's* women braced arms with Walili, and walked her to the *choza* of her parents. When her father and mother came out to see the commotion, they could not believe their eyes.

"Watili," her father said, "How could you return?"

As he held the palms of her hands, he noticed the scars around her wrists and the scar on her neck. He remembered the days the young were abducted and hog-tied to an aspen tree. Her mother gave her a loving hug, and tears of both women could not stop flowing.

Watili looked at the village; much was the same, but the sadness and emptiness on the faces of the families was evident for the loss of the young people that day. A sadness hung over the villagers: losing their young adults was a shock. How had it been possible? A disbelief about such a loss still overshadowed the happiness amongst the villagers. How was it the *Apaches* had found them in this discrete location, when it had never happened before? Watili knew the answer, and she thought to herself: *I brought the reason for this unhappiness, and I left him at the entrance to my village.*

Watili did not forget that *Cibolero* was at the entrance to the village, and asked her parents and the group to wait one minute. She quickly ran to the entrance. *Cibolero* was very nervous and scared from the commotion of her arrival.

"You are still here. Good. Come with me, we will find you a safe place to relax," Watili said.

Watili walked with *Cibolero* into the village: not a normal sight in these lands. She walked him to the front of her parents *choza,* and told her parents he'd helped to bring her back home. She requested privacy for *Cibolero* in one of the empty *chozas* next to her parents. She also told the group that *Cibolero* would return later with another man. *Cibolero* entered the *choza*. There was firewood next to the opening, used to create warmth inside the reed hut.

Watili entered the large *choza* of her parents, and they sat down to talk around the small fire, her parents still amazed about her arrival. Her father, the *Cacique* of the band, and was speechless. Her mother asked, "How are you?" as she looked at the scars on her body.

"I am fine, Mama. They made me slave for a family whom I lived with. They taught me to understand and write the language of that land, Spanish. I took care of the home and their young children, and was treated as one of their family," Watili explained.

"Your brother? Paregrue?" her father asked.

"I have not seen or heard anything of him. He was taken to work and labor in the silver mines in a place called *Janos*," Watili said.

"Do you think he is alive?" her father asked.

Watili did not answer.

"When I was with the Spanish, I was asked to clean an office of a man by the name of Don Bernardo Pacheco y Mierra. When I was in his office, I saw a map on his table. I looked closely at this map, and I recognized our village. He had writings of how to arrive here. This man is with us; he is at the distant entryway to the village," Watili explained.

"This man of authority, why did he complete this lengthy journey?" her father asked.

"He is the man who can give me freedom, and the man who had the foresight to return me to my village. He paid a premium to the Spanish family for my freedom," Watili explained.

"Why would he do this?" her father asked.

"He wants the location of the gold and silver ore," Watili said bluntly. "Yet, I have an idea to share with you."

Her father's face grew sad and sullen.

"I need to ask *Cibolero* to go and get this man. He is with animals that have long legs, and I do not want to scare the villagers," Watili explained.

"You know how to mount those animals?" her mother asked. "You have learned much."

Watili got up and walked outside to find *Cibolero*. She called for him.

"*Cibolero*, are you ready to get Don Bernardo before it gets dark? Do you know your way?"

Cibolero exited the *choza* and said, "Yes, I know the pathway; I will go get him."

"Listen, when you arrive close to the village, dismount and walk in. You know what horses mean to natives: not freedom, but slavery."

"Yes, I understand." *Cibolero* scurried to locate Don Bernardo and return before nightfall.

Watili's mother noticed these directives and said, "You the *Cacaqui* here!" and laughed, surprised at the directives given to the white man.

Two hours later, as the sun began to set, the men appeared walking their horses into the village. Most villagers had never seen a horse, and marveled at such an animal that could carry a person to another village or to hunt for deer and elk. Almost all members of the band touched the horses, and were stunned at the strength and mass of these beasts.

The men walked their horses to the front of Watili's parents *choza* as she walked out. She said to them, "You can tie the horses to the tree grove behind these huts. They can feed on the grass and water by the small *rito* that flows there. I will meet you in *Cibolero's choza* in a little while."

After the men retired to the *choza*, Watili entered and addressed Don Bernardo directly.

"I am grateful you have given me the freedom to return home. As you have kept your word, I will keep mine. Tomorrow, mid-morning, I will show you the gold and silver veins. I will not show you how to get there, for it will forever change this area. I cannot do that to my community. I will ask my older brother to accompany us. This will be interesting, for he has never seen a horse."

"*Cibolero*, will you help my brother learn to ride in the early morning? Watili asked.

"Yes," he answered.

"Don Bernardo, do you understand why I cannot show you the pathway to the veins? Watili asked.

"I understand the danger I have given your community," Don Bernardo said.

All retired for the evening. Don Bernardo and *Cibolero* were relieved they would not be harmed.

At sunrise, Watili awoke *Cibolero*. He arose, placed the saddles upon the horses, and led them to the pasture. Many of the band heard this noise and awoke to see what was going on.

Watili introduced her older brother Natim to *Cibolero*.

"*Cibolero* will show you how to get in the saddle, use reins, and direct this horse."

Natim was very nervous; he put his hand on the backside of the horse to feel its strength. The horse knew immediately this man was afraid of him. *Cibolero* then showed him how to mount the saddle, and mounted a different beast as an example.

Natim having watched this, placed his right barefoot in the stirrup, swung his left foot above the horse's head, and mounted the horse. Natim raised his head, thinking he was a real *vaquero*. The whole village laughed, for he'd mounted backward and was facing the backside of the horse.

Cibolero helped him off and showed him again: this time the correct way. Natim grabbed the reins. *Cibolero* told him to kick gently with his heels to make the beast go forward. Natim did this and for a short while rode—until the horse wanted to show him who is boss. The gallop caused Natim to fall off the horse, and the band laughed again. This was done a few times; the villagers loved this comedy routine.

Finally, Natim got it, and began managing the horse himself.

By mid-morning, Watili, Natim, and Don Bernardo were on horses. The band wondered at the control and freedom Watili possessed over the strength of the horse, as she controlled with grace this beast—as if she were his master. The three left the village saying, "We will ride slowly, as to not lose Natim."

After riding one half of an hour, and the village not in sight, Watili ordered her brother to come forward. He took a thick and wide strip out of his waistband, and Watili told Don Bernardo, "We will take you to the veins; we will blindfold you."

Don Bernardo nodded 'yes'. Now he could see only darkness, and only feel the direction of his horse.

In the meantime, *Cibolero* stayed at the village. The *Cacique* gave him permission to walk around the village. He looked at working systems such as the tanning of deer, rabbits, and hares to make long sleeve shirts, pants, and coats for all the villagers.

The only problem was that after he walked by a system, some young women saw him in his *chaleco* (vest) and leather pants, as well as the red, curly hair under his cowboy hat. They left their posts to follow him along with other young women. The mothers yelled at them to return, but knew the giggles about a rare sight take precedence over work. Funny how *Cibolero* had this effect on women, wherever he traveled.

Watili rode another hour and one half. Don Bernardo thought: *this vein is very far from the village*. However, the vein was no more than fifteen minutes from the village, in a discreet cavern of high cliffs and high trees. They arrived at the flat patch a short distance from the narrow opening to the cavern and dismounted.

Don Bernardo thought to himself: *this better be some vein*.

As the group walked up the hillside to the high rocks, they slid between two flatirons, then another, and finally another to enter the cavern. They removed the blindfold from Don Bernardo.

He opened his eyes and could not believe what he saw; the cavern was striped in gold and silver veins that would make discoveries in far-off places in India and Africa seem meager.

Finally, Don Bernardo with his European arrogance, position on slavery, and map-making skills was speechless.

"I brought you here because I listened to you on the trail. You talked about the delicate and innocent balance of the natives, the beauty of the land, and finally, you did not disclose the *Rio de San Colorado* (Colorado River) is a passageway to the west coast. If you are genuine in your words, you will know a European gold rush will enter these lands, and the people and land will forever be stamped out. But I wanted you to know," Watili explained.

"I do not know what to say," said Don Bernardo.

"It is for you to learn, not to say. We enjoy being dependent on the land, many times we act as One. *Cibolero* is right, we are entwined with Nature; we are One with Nature. It is this dependency that brings our souls close to the Creator," Watili explained.

"Your ways will eventually destroy this land and water. Your people will roll right over my people, its places, and its values. Your people will never know yourselves if you do not know those who came before you. That is what I want you to learn," Watili railed into Don Bernardo.

"As those green lights came upon us and scared us, that intelligence knows there is but One God and it may not be their God, but they wanted our reaction. God created this one land for us to cherish, not exploit!" Watili flat-out explained to Don Bernardo.

Don Bernardo was humbled and finally understood. With all the riches within their grasp, they did not want gold and silver. Rather, the relationship with Nature was their priority.

Natim then put the blindfold on Don Bernardo, and they slowly walked out of the cavern to mount their horses for the long horseback ride to the village.

As they arrived outside of the village, Natim removed the blindfold. Don Bernardo looked back, not sure where he had been.

Cibolero met the group and curiously asked, "Did you find the vein?"

Don Bernardo just shook his head and walked back to his *choza*.

As nightfall arrived, Watili and her brother entered her parent's *choza* and sat by the fire.

"I trusted you today; did you show the stranger the vein?" asked her father.

"We did, but we blindfolded him so he does not know the location," Watili said.

"Very intelligent. I see you have grown up, and we are lucky to have you back," her father said.

"Are you going to stay?" her mother asked.

"Yes, I have been given my freedom. We must allow the two men to leave. They have kept their word to me," said Watili.

"The *cibolero* with red hair: he seems of a different sprit," her father remarked.

"That is what the *Cacique* of the *Cosinanas* Band said," Watili said. "That is what I want to talk to you about. On this journey, I learned much."

"Tell me," her father said.

"The *Cosinanas* Band is not that far from here, yet they have permanent structures made of mud and stone, corrals to hold domestic herds, and storage structures for drying vegetables, fruits, and medicinal plants and roots."

"Tell me more," her father said.

"We need to adopt these skills to survive. This way, our braves can learn to defend our village, instead of doing chores all day, not prepared for attacks that are sure to come." Watili explained, as she was an example of a raid that had changed her life.

Her father looked at her. He said, "We could visit them, we are not in any disagreements with that band. We must take gifts to show our sincerity. They would be interested in your story."

"I will talk with the strangers this evening. I will thank them for the journey, and tell them tomorrow morning is a good time to leave.

I will ask them to not disclose our location. I do not feel we can ask any more of them. They will not leave the animal with the long legs behind," Watili said.

"That is fine with me," her father said. He did not understand the value of horses as of yet.

Watili got up and walked to the *choza* of *Cibolero* and Don Bernardo, and sat by the fire in their hut.

"Don Bernardo tells me of the vein; it is quite a view," said *Cibolero*.

"Yes, quite a view. You both are free to leave tomorrow early in the morning; it's probably the safest time to leave. I want to thank you, Don Bernardo, for giving me my freedom and bringing me home," Watili said.

"Your strength, wisdom, and honesty was something to behold," said Don Bernardo. "You handled all of this in a manner that shows leadership and wisdom."

"*Cibolero*, sometimes leaving pushes the truth to the forefront. I must admit I have been sweet on you since you were healing in the *choza* by the river."

Finally admitting to herself her feelings toward him, and finally acknowledging his hazel green eyes, reminded her of the opulent green jade her grandfather had brought back after a lengthy journey. "My life is here with my family," Watili said, in all earnestness of her feelings.

Cibolero smiled for he understood the situation, "Maybe you will travel to El Paso. You know how to travel now and speak and write in Spanish. You could visit," he said with a chuckle. "Yet, I want to thank you for teaching us the about the Oneness between Man and Nature, and how God wants this relationship to exist—and for the land to not be exploited."

"You do get it, *Cibolero*. I will miss you," she said, as tears rolled down her lovely cheek.

"Don Bernardo," she started, as she shook her head and could not look at him. "The map you drew and wrote will create massive injury upon natives wherever you have traveled. You may be a hero to your European people, but to natives, you have exposed them to be exploited and stamped out. I have not told my father, for he would not allow you to leave. Do you understand what you have done?

Don Bernardo said nothing.

Watili walked out.

As daybreak arose the next morning, *Cibolero* and Don Bernardo arose and prepared their horses to be saddled, fed, and given water before leaving.

Watili awoke. Almost all of her village was still sleeping on this cold morning.

Watili walked over to *Cibolero*, and hugged and kissed him on the cheek.

She just looked at Don Bernardo and hoped he'd learned from the events he'd witnessed. She hoped he would never do it again. The men walked their horses to the entrance of the village, and then mounted their horses, with the third horse in tow, and rode off.

Watili the Leader

Watili returned to her parents' *choza,* and began speaking with her mother and father.

"You have seen and learned so much, Daughter," the father said.

"That is why I have returned. I arrive as a forewarning that our village must adjust to these newcomers if we are to survive as a community." Watili's dire warning sent chills down her parents' spines.

"The Spanish want two items: gold and silver ore, and Indian labor to extract this ore. They will use other native bands like the *Apaches* to assist them in obtaining items or will come themselves to obtain these items," Watili explained.

"We have heard nothing from your brother, Peregrue," her mother said sorrowfully.

"We have been attacked before. Other native bands have come at us, and we have fought and survived," the father proudly declared.

"Yes, you and our braves fought and won. Yet you have not seen the advanced armaments, metals, and iron the Spanish can bring to wage war. I have seen their large, powerful fire sticks in *El Paso*. We do not possess that capability," Watili said.

"Where are these Spanish from?" the mother asked.

"They come from another land, and they cross mighty waters in a vessel of wood; that is how they arrive. They bring weapons from their home lands to wage these wars," Watili explained. "We must learn to use wheels—wooden discs—to which are mounted a flat board that allow you to move items effectively both to and from locations. We must become a village that can move quickly and maintain our harvests."

"How is this to be done?" the father asked.

"We can build pens out of wooden stakes to hold wild turkeys and mountain goats; we can build cages for rabbits. The wooden stakes can also provide a location for planting small gardens of vegetables and medicinal plants, you know, the ones that Grandfather scours the area for to be used for his remedies. This I saw at the *Guapi* Band."

"If this is to work, what will we do with our young men?" the father asked. "They normally dig up plants and vegetables. They hunt deer."

"The men will still hunt for deer and wild game, but by growing those plants and vegetables in gardens, the young men will now have time to train for defense of our village," Watili explained. "At one of the villages we visited, I envision we can expect to see *Apache* among them. The *Apache* may have been bartering with the villagers, but he could also have been an informant, gathering information on the next village so his band could plan for another slave raid."

"How would we know such information?" the father asked.

"We'll send out scouts to learn of such threats. This would prevent surprise attacks from both the *Apaches* and the Spanish. We would have to move our village under such an imminent threat."

"If we use this wheel and flat board to move to a previously unidentified, new location," the suspicious father said, "What will pull this contraption?"

"We will have to trade for horses, otherwise we are at a great disadvantage," Watili admitted.

"What do we possess that could be traded to obtain such beasts?" The father's brow darkened in thought.

"We will need to learn to mine the silver and gold that is in the rock veins, the ones I took Don Bernardo to see," Watili explained. "I have now seen two such operations on the journey here."

The father felt dumfounded; this vision for survival was much broader in concept then he had imagined. He said slowly, "These horses, when not at work digging ore, could assist us in the village to complete heavy work." He smiled as he wrapped his mind around these concepts. His eyes met his daughter's as he asked, "Your ability to speak Spanish would allow us to barter. If we carved out this ore the Spanish demand, where could the exchange take place?"

"The *Ohkey Owngeh* Band, a four-day horse ride south from *Parussi*, holds an annual slave fair. There, horses and other goods of all types are exchanged. Many *Ute* Tribes participate in this fair," Watili explained.

And so it was.

The visionary ideas that Watili had expressed were presented to *Parussi's* Council of Elders, and many of her thoughts were implemented to create a mobile village for the band. Watili and her bilingual skills were used to barter and secure horses that revolutionized both working and living conditions in *Parussi*. Watili's efforts immortalized her as the *Parussi's* Visionary Leader, forever remembered by her *Parussi* village as willing to use her bartering skills for their salvation.

The *Utes* became one of first Native American bands to secure and use horses in everyday life, as well as in times of war.

Final Chapter

As Don Bernardo and *Cibolero* headed back to *El Paso*, they knew better than to take the short-cut through the pass to *Wahuataya*, otherwise known as La Veta Pass, and run into the Apaches again. They were reminded of the green lights that appeared in the evening camp on that night so long ago.

Don Bernardo said, "Remember when those green lights appeared and scared us? You yelled 'Save me Abraham.'"

Cibolero answered, "I do recall the green lights, though I do not see any lights this evening."

Don Bernardo asked, "Where did you say you came into this territory of New Spain?"

"My family was part of the original expedition with Don Juan Oñate in 1598," The *Cibolero* said proudly.

"*Perdona* me-Excuse me—I don't even know your name," Don Bernardo answered.

"My name is Juan Gallegos del llano," *Cibolero* answered. "I am called *del llano*—from the prairie—for we have hunted buffalo on the prairie for some time now. I just kept the term so people know where I am from."

"Yet when those green lights appeared, you yelled *Abraham!*" Don Bernardo pressed, knowing well of the exodus and history of the Inquisition from Spain.

"You are correct," *Cibolero* answered.

"That would mean that some of the first *vaqueros*—cowboys—in this territory were Jewish," Don Bernardo assessed.

Cibolero smiled. "Yes, some of the first cowboys were Jewish. You know, Don B, you also keep secrets. You did not disclose the western passage at the deep river at *Rio de San Colorado*—Saint Colorado river. You know that if that passage was disclosed, the Crown would have immediately sent another expedition to unite this continent of the high mountains to the Pacific Ocean. Why did you do this?" he asked.

"I did not want these unspoiled lands exploited. The beauty of these lands is unsurpassable," Don Bernardo answered.

"Yet you still want the silver industry to exist?" *Cibolero* asked with caution.

"Are you going to go into those deep and dangerous mines to split rock with a pick axe?" Don Bernardo asked Cibolero.

The vaquero did not answer.

"The Crown will not send the Spanish or other Europeans into such a dangerous work place. The only option is to send the Indian slaves—*esclavos*—into the mines. I understand most of them will not live."

"Yet, you have seen Watili, and she was intelligent, educable, learning to read and write. She has a soul," *Cibolero* said emotionally. "I learned that her ability to meld Nature with her prayers is spiritual healing. This is what the Creator wanted man to learn and to have reverence for."

"Yes, I have learned that from her. She is possibly a rarity. Most Indians do not possess that level of leaning capability," Don Bernardo answered.

Cibolero sighed. "I no longer feel Indians should be forced to go into the mines. I never believed in slavery yet I never objected to the existence of the silver mines."

"I'm not so sure there are more Watilis in the *rancherias*," said Don B.

"Yet with your own eyes you witnessed a wonder: she possessed advanced knowledge about the fusion of natural healing and spiritual prayer. Can the Christian doctors do this?" *Cibolero* demanded, knowing that Watili saved his life with her knowledge. "She gained this ability from her grandfather and mother. There must be others with that kind of learning."

"I am still in awe of how she saved your life. She blended organic Nature with her spiritual prayers to preserve your life. I had never before witnessed such a thing," Don Bernardo acknowledged.

"Watili united Mother Earth with spirituality to heal and give life. That is what the Creator, intended: for man to coexist with Nature. It is the highest level of respect and intelligence given to the Creator," *Cibolero* explained. "This is what the Creator intended for us to understand—Nature, this *world*, was created to connect to the spirituality to God itself."

"Yes, Watili has moved my sentiment for the native. I don't know how to comprehend her knowledge," Don Bernardo confessed.

"Then why do you enslave these people, these individual souls?" *Cibolero* asked forcefully.

"Because I know of no other way to extract the silver ore, *esclavos*—slaves—must do this work. All of this to appease the Crown!" Don Bernardo blurted out as his eyes burned with emotion.

"And where is that ore sent to? Who does it benefit? New Spain?" *Cibolero* asked.

"The ore benefits the areas around the mines somewhat; I have seen that with my eyes, but I think the Crown garnishes most of the benefit," Don Bernardo admitted.

"I think that this ore is funding the beginning of the war with the British." The *Cibolero* pondered the developments of such a war before drifting back to the topic. "I do not believe the average person in old Spain receives the benefit of the Mexican silver mines."

"I see your points, but they do not change my position on development of the silver industry in Mexico," Don Bernardo said.

"Where does that leave us? Watili has shown she is equal to us, yet she possesses this healing knowledge of the Creator that you and I do not," *Cibolero* said.

"Do you think her wisdom of Nature will be accepted or used by the educated minds of Europe or our western medical doctors?" Don Bernardo asked.

Cibolero looked down at his horse, "No, likely not. Only two *vaqueros* and many Indians have lived with this form of medical healing for centuries," *Cibolero* said, bitterly disappointedly. "But there must be a way to share this knowledge of Nature's healing and prayer?"

"Possibly, Watili's healing ability only works in Nature. Have you thought of this?" Don Bernardo asked. "The Creator made Nature and gave great healing skills. Perhaps they work jointly only in their organic environment."

"Why would the Creator, not want this knowledge shared? This was intended for us to understand. This world was created to connect to the spirituality of God himself," *Cibolero* stated.

"You were given life and felt Watili's healing spirituality. Not everyone has gone through that, yet I did witness this feat. The Christian friars and priests will not even know what we are talking about when we get back," Don Bernardo explained. "Maybe you should accept that what we have seen was the experience of two Europeans…

two pale skins…two outsiders who were given a rare glimpse into the Oneness of God and Nature."

"I am moved by this experience." *Cibolero* spoke softly.

"My knowledge of the spiritual realm has awoken. Watili is special. You should have married her!" Don Bernardo said, laughing.

"It did cross my mind." *Cibolero* laughed as they continued their journey back to El Paso.

Other Books and Sites by Anthony Garcia

The Portal of Light   www.ThePortalLight.com

Shared Lives, Twin Sun   www.SharedLivesTwinSun.com

Alabados   www.Alabados.com

Made in the USA
San Bernardino, CA
30 January 2018